Old Friends
and
Lasting Favorites

This book belongs to
"Little Jim" Barbarick
born, May 20-1959
passed away Feb. 28-1964

VOLUME 4

THE
GOLDEN TREASURY
OF
CHILDREN'S LITERATURE

Old Friends and

EDITED AND SELECTED

ILLUSTRATED BY WILLIAM DUGAN

ROBERT J. LEE ELOISE WILKIN

J. P. MILLER GORDON LAITE

KANAKO TANABE W. T. MARS

MAE GERHARD LOWELL HESS

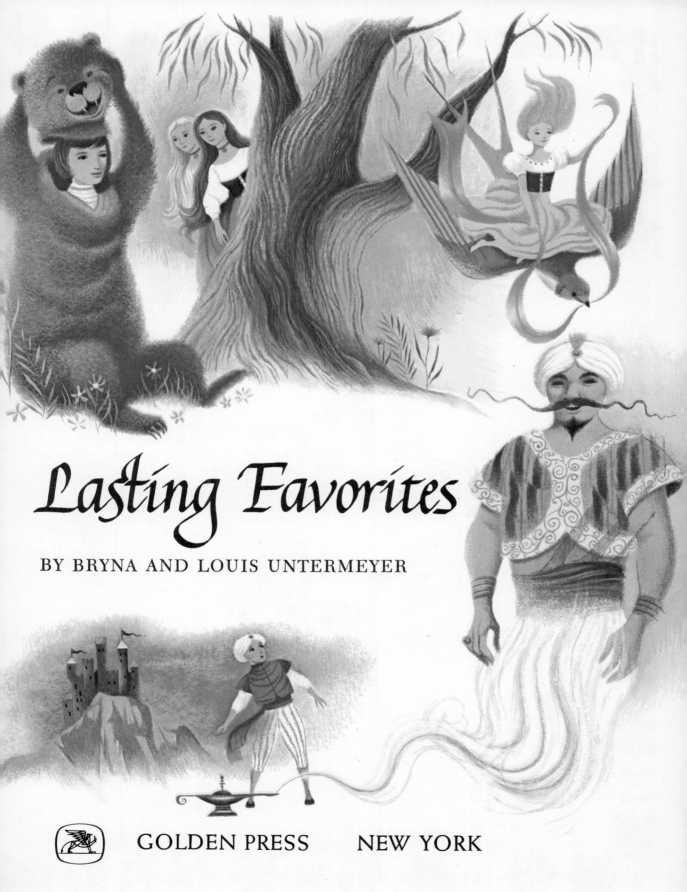

Lasting Favorites

BY BRYNA AND LOUIS UNTERMEYER

GOLDEN PRESS   NEW YORK

ACKNOWLEDGMENTS: *The editors and publisher have made every effort to trace the ownership of all copyrighted material and to secure permission from the holders of the copyright. In the event of any question arising as to the use of any of the selections, the publisher and editors, while expressing regret for inadvertent error, will be happy to make necessary corrections in future printings. Thanks are due to the following publishers, publications, agents, and authors for permission to reprint the material indicated.*

LONGMANS, GREEN AND COMPANY for the version of "Aladdin" from *Arabian Nights* by Andrew Lang.

LOUIS UNTERMEYER for the adaptation of "Puss in Boots," "Blue-Beard," and "Hop O'-My-Thumb" by Charles Perrault, from *The French Fairy Tales*, published by Didier. Copyright 1946.

The editors acknowledge with thanks the help of Norma Anchin Untermeyer and the painstaking assistance of Millie Isaacs in the preparation of the manuscript.

CONTENTS

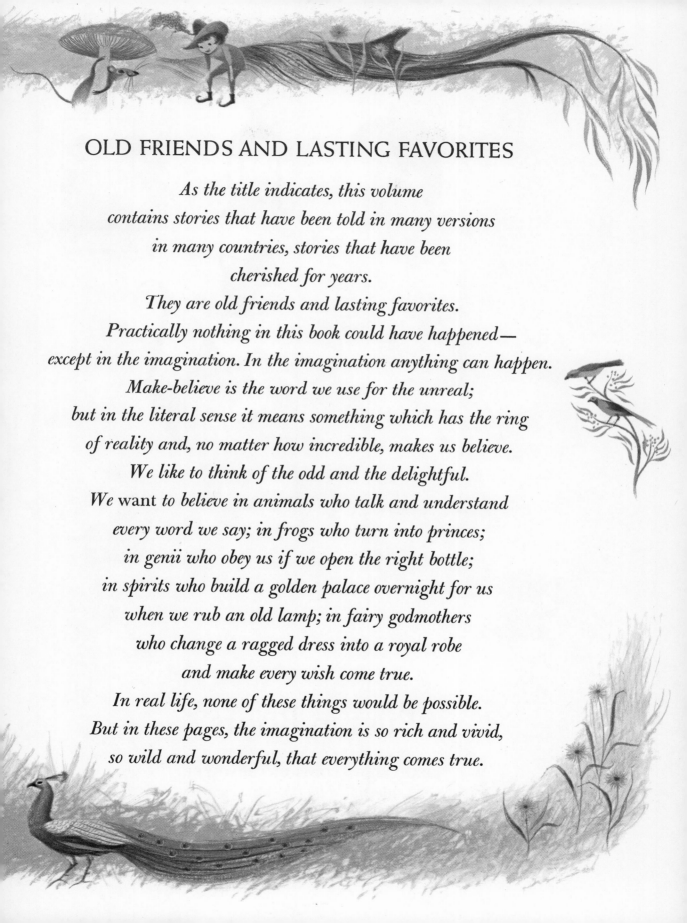

OLD FRIENDS AND LASTING FAVORITES

As the title indicates, this volume
contains stories that have been told in many versions
in many countries, stories that have been
cherished for years.
They are old friends and lasting favorites.
Practically nothing in this book could have happened—
except in the imagination. In the imagination anything can happen.
Make-believe is the word we use for the unreal;
but in the literal sense it means something which has the ring
of reality and, no matter how incredible, makes us believe.
We like to think of the odd and the delightful.
We want to believe in animals who talk and understand
every word we say; in frogs who turn into princes;
in genii who obey us if we open the right bottle;
in spirits who build a golden palace overnight for us
when we rub an old lamp; in fairy godmothers
who change a ragged dress into a royal robe
and make every wish come true.
In real life, none of these things would be possible.
But in these pages, the imagination is so rich and vivid,
so wild and wonderful, that everything comes true.

Puss in Boots

BY CHARLES PERRAULT
ADAPTED BY LOUIS UNTERMEYER
Illustrated by J. P. MILLER

There was once a miller who was so poor that when he died he had
nothing to leave his three sons but his mill, his ass, and his cat.
These things were quickly shared by the sons—no lawyer was needed
to settle the estate. The eldest son took the mill, the second took the
ass, and so the third and youngest received nothing but the cat. Really,
he was not very happy about it.

"My brothers," said he to himself, "may make a living by joining
forces. But what can I do? Even if I eat the cat and make a muff of its
skin, I still will have to die of hunger."

The cat, who pretended not to have been listening, heard all this.
He spoke up seriously:

"Don't worry, master. Just get me a bag, and have a pair of little boots made for me. Then you will see that I'm not such a bad bargain, after all."

The cat's master did not expect much. But he had seen how clever the cat was catching rats and mice—he had noticed how he had hung by his heels, pretending he was dead, or hid himself in the flour-bin—so he was not without hope that something good would come of it.

14

After the cat had received what he asked for, he pulled on the little boots and strutted around in them. Then he put the bag around his neck, holding the string between his two front paws, and went to a piece of ground where there were large numbers of rabbits. He put some bran and lettuce in the bag, and stretched himself out pretending he was dead.

The sly puss had just settled himself when things worked out according to plan. A frisky and foolish young rabbit put his head into the bag and started to nibble the food. Puss immediately pulled the string tight and had his catch.

Proud of his prize, he went straight to the king's palace and asked to speak to his majesty. He was ushered into the royal apartment, where he bowed low and said to the king:

"Your majesty, I have brought you a rabbit from the fields of my master, the marquis of Carabas"—for that was the title which puss had conferred upon his master.

"Tell your master," said the king, "that I thank him, and that I am pleased with his gift."

Sometime later, puss hid himself among tall grain, a place much visited by birds. He held his bag open until a couple of partridges flew

in. Again he went to the palace and presented the birds to the king, who received them with even greater pleasure, and gave the cat a little present for himself.

The cat continued doing this sort of thing for two or three months, each time taking game to the king as a gift from his master. Finally, there came a day when the cat learned that the king was to go for an outing along the riverside with his daughter, the most beautiful princess in the world.

It was then that the cat said to his master, "The time has come. If you do what I tell you, your fortune is made. All you have to do is bathe in the river, at a spot which I shall point out to you. Leave the rest to me."

The young man had no idea what was going to happen, but he did exactly what puss had advised. While he was bathing, the king came along and the cat cried out:

"Help! help! My lord marquis of Carabas is drowning!"

At these cries the king stuck his head out of the carriage window. He recognized the cat who had brought him so many appetizing gifts, and commanded his guards to hurry to the aid of the marquis of Carabas.

While they were helping the poor marquis out of the river, the cat came up to the carriage and told the king that, while his master was bathing, some robbers had stolen his clothes, although he had tried to stop them by calling, "Stop, thief!" at the top of his voice. (The cunning cat had hidden the clothes under a stone.)

The king received the young man with great kindness, and immediately ordered the officers of his wardrobe to run and bring one of his finest suits for the marquis of Carabas. The rich clothes fit him extremely well, for he was a handsome fellow, and the king's daughter took an instant fancy to him. In fact the young man had looked at her shyly but tenderly only a few times before she was completely in love with him.

The king insisted that the young marquis enter the carriage and drive with them. The cat, delighted with the way his scheme was working

out, went on ahead. Soon he came to a place where some farmers were mowing a meadow, and he said to them:

"My good people, be sure to tell the king that the meadow you are mowing belongs to the marquis of Carabas. If you don't, you will be chopped into mincemeat."

Just as the cat had expected, when the carriage came along, the king asked the mowers to whom the meadow belonged.

"To my lord marquis of Carabas," replied the mowers, for they were taking no chances at the cat's threat.

"You have a very fine estate here," said the king to the marquis.

"You can see for yourself, your majesty," replied the young man. "This meadow yields a rich harvest every year."

Still keeping ahead of the carriage, the cat saw some reapers in a field, and said to them:

"My good people, be sure to tell the king that the field you are reaping belongs to the marquis of Carabas. If you don't, you will be chopped into mincemeat."

A few minutes later the king passed by and asked who was the owner of all the fields.

"My lord marquis of Carabas," replied the reapers.

The cat, still going ahead of the royal carriage, told everyone he met to say the same thing, and the king was amazed at the size of the estate of the young marquis of Carabas.

Puss came at last to a large castle, owned by the richest ogre ever known, for all the land which the king had passed belonged to this ogre. The cat had already found out who this ogre was, and what magic things he could do. So he asked to speak with him, saying that he wished to pay his respects to so rich and great a magician. The ogre received him politely—at least as politely as an ogre could—and asked him to sit down.

"They tell me," said the cat, "that you have the power to change yourself into all sorts of animals; that you can, for example, turn yourself into a lion or an elephant."

"That is true," said the ogre gruffly, "and to prove it I shall now turn into a lion."

The cat was so frightened at the sight of a lion so close to him that he scrambled onto the roof—and it was none too easy for him, because his boots were not meant for walking on such a slippery surface. Soon the ogre turned himself back, and puss confessed that he had been terrified.

"Had I not seen that, I would not have believed it. But," continued the cat, "I've also been told that you have the still greater power to change yourself into the shape of little animals—that you can, for example, change yourself into a rat or even a small mouse. That must be quite impossible."

"Impossible!" growled the ogre. "You shall see!" At the same time the ogre transformed himself into a mouse and scurried about the floor. The next moment puss pounced upon him and quickly ate him up.

A little later the king came along, saw the magnificent castle, and wished to visit it. Puss, hearing the carriage rumble across the drawbridge, ran out and said:

"Welcome, your majesty, welcome to the castle of my lord marquis of Carabas."

"What! My dear marquis!" cried the king. "Does this castle also belong to you? Nothing I have seen is finer than this courtyard and the stately building around it. Let us look at the inside, if you please."

The marquis gave his hand to the princess and followed the king, who went first. They passed into a huge hall where a magnificent feast had been spread by the ogre for certain friends of his. The other ogres were afraid to enter the castle now that the king was there.

The king was won over by the charm and fine figure of the marquis. As for his daughter, the young princess had fallen madly in love with

him. So, having drunk five or six glasses of wine, and seeing the vast estate all about him, the king said:

"My dear marquis, if you wish to be my son-in-law—it rests entirely with you."

Bowing very low, the marquis accepted the honor bestowed upon him. The very same day he was married to the princess.

Puss became a person of great importance at court. Never again did he chase a mouse—except for fun.

Blue-Beard

BY CHARLES PERRAULT
ADAPTED BY LOUIS UNTERMEYER
Illustrated by KANAKO TANABE

Once upon a time there was a very rich man, who had town and country houses and lived in a magnificent castle. He had great quantities of gold and silver, and precious stones and rich furniture, and great gilded coaches. But he was hideously ugly, and what made him most disagreeable was that he had an enormous blue beard, which looked so strange and frightful that all the ladies ran away from him.

One of his neighbors, a fine lady, had two very handsome daughters. Blue-Beard asked for one in marriage, leaving the lady to choose which she would give him. The daughters did not like him at all, neither being able to make up her mind to marry a man who had a blue beard. What made them like him even less was that he had already married several wives, and nobody knew what had become of them.

To become better acquainted, Blue-Beard invited them, with their mother and some young people of the neighborhood, to his castle, where they stayed eight whole days.

They spent their time walking, hunting, fishing, dancing and feasting. They played games and stayed up most of the night. At last all went on so well that the younger daughter began to think that the master of the house was not such a bad fellow after all, and that his beard was not really so blue. In fact before the week was ended, she had consented to become his wife.

At the end of a month, Blue-Beard told his wife that he must go away for at least six weeks on important business. He wished her to enjoy herself while he was away, to invite some of her friends, and to live as happily as possible.

"Here," said he, "are the keys of the two great storerooms. Here are those for the gold and silver plate, which is not used every day. Here are the keys of my strongboxes where I keep my gold and silver. Here are the keys of my caskets, where I keep my jewels. And here is the master-key to all the rooms. But this little key is to the small room at the end of the passage on the ground floor. Examine everything; go everywhere you wish—but I forbid you to open this one little room. And I warn you that if you disobey, your punishment will be more severe than you can imagine."

She promised strictly to obey everything he had commanded, and he set out on his journey.

The friends and neighbors did not wait long for an invitation to call upon the young wife. They were eager to see all the splendors of her house, not having dared to come

while her husband was there, because his blue beard frightened them. They were soon running through the chambers, closets, and store-rooms, each of which seemed richer than the others. They went upstairs to the wardrobes, where they admired the number and beauty of the tapestries, the stately beds, the elegant sofas, the tastefully carved stands and tables, the shining mirrors where they could see themselves from head to foot, and the frames of which, made of gold and silver, were handsomer than any they had ever seen before. They did not cease to praise and admire the good fortune of their friend. But she was not as pleased as the others at seeing all these fine things, because she was longing to examine the small room on the ground floor.

At length her curiosity became so great that, without considering how impolite it was to leave her company alone, she hurried down the back staircase, with such eager haste that she was more than once in danger of breaking her neck.

She was almost breathless when she reached the threshold of the chamber, and a sudden fear seemed to check her as she called to mind the ominous warning of her husband, and the terrible punishment he might inflict if he discovered her disobedience. But the temptation was so strong that she could not resist it. She seized the little key and, with a trembling hand, opened the door.

On entering the room, she at first saw nothing, as the shutters were closed. But on opening them and admitting the daylight, a frightful spectacle met her view. The floor was covered with blood, and along the walls were strung up the bodies of several murdered women. "These, then," she thought in her agony, "are those former wives of Blue-Beard who so mysteriously disappeared." Almost fainting with terror, she tried to replace the key in the lock from which she had withdrawn it on entering, but her hand was so unsteady that it fell upon the floor of the apartment. Hastily picking it up and locking the door, she hurried to her own chamber, and tried to compose herself. But the shock had been so terrible that it took a long time. To add to her worry, she now perceived that the key, which had fallen, was stained with blood. She washed it with soap, and scoured it with sand and stone. But the

blood would not come off; it remained as visible as ever. The truth was, though she did not know it, that the key was a magic key, so that when the stains were gone from one side, they would reappear on the other.

Blue-Beard unexpectedly returned from his journey the same evening, and said that he had received letters telling him that the business which had taken him from home had been settled in his favor. His wife tried to appear as if nothing had disturbed her, as if she were really over-joyed at seeing him so soon again. The following morning her fears were suddenly reawakened when Blue-Beard demanded his keys. After hesitating a moment, she produced them; but her husband remarked that her hand trembled as she gave them to him, and he at once guessed what had happened.

"How is it, my dear," he said, very politely, "that the key of the little room is not among the rest?"

"Isn't it?" she replied, as if surprised. "I must have left it upstairs on my table."

"Be so good as to fetch it, then, without delay," said Blue-Beard, with forced calmness.

After many delays and excuses she was forced to bring him the key. He examined it carefully. Then, eyeing her very sternly, he asked, "How is it, madam, that I see blood-stains on the key?"

"I know nothing about it," she faltered, turning pale.

"You know nothing about it, eh, madam?" returned Blue-Beard, with a sneer. "Then I shall tell you all about it. You determined to pay a visit to the forbidden little room. Very well. You shall visit it again, and at once! And you will take your place with the women you found there."

She threw herself at his feet, and, weeping bitterly, begged for forgiveness. But all in vain.

"If I *must* die, then," said she, looking at him with tearful eyes, "give me a little time to say my prayers." She was so beautiful and sorrowful, she would have melted a rock. But Blue-Beard's heart was harder than any stone.

"I will give you," he said, "exactly one quarter of an hour, but not a moment more."

As soon as she was alone, she called out to her sister, and said, "Sister Anne, go up, I pray you, to the top of the tower, and see if my brothers are coming. They promised me they would come to visit me today. And if you see them, give them a signal to hasten."

Her sister went up to the top of the tower, and the wife called out: "Anne, sister Anne, do you see anybody coming?"

And her sister replied: "I see nothing but the burning sun and the waving grass."

Meantime, Blue-Beard, holding a great cutlass, cried out at the top of his voice: "Come down at once or I shall come after you."

"Just one moment more," cried his wife; and then called very softly: "Anne, sister Anne, do you see anybody coming?"

"I see," replied sister Anne, "a great cloud of dust, which is moving this way."

"Is it my brothers?"

"Alas, no, my sister; it is a flock of sheep."

"Will you come down?" shouted Blue-Beard.

"Only one moment more," she cried; and then called out: "Anne, sister Anne, do you see anybody coming?"

"I see two horsemen coming this way but they are yet very far off."

"Thank God!" she cried out. "They are my brothers!"

"I will give them a signal to hasten," said her sister.

Blue-Beard now cried out so loud that the whole house trembled. His terrified wife came down, and threw herself at his feet, weeping, her hair tumbling over her shoulders.

"It's no use," said he. "You must die." Then, taking her by the hair with one hand, and raising his cutlass in the other, he was about to cut off her head. Turning tearful eyes upon him, she begged him to give her one more moment to recover herself. "Not an instant," roared Blue-Beard. He raised his arm, but there came so loud a knocking at the gate that he stopped short. The gate was thrown open and two horsemen rushed in brandishing swords, and flew furiously at Blue-Beard. He recognized them as the brothers of his wife, and tried to make his escape. But before he could do so, they fell upon him, and ran their swords through his body.

Blue-Beard had no heirs, and so his wife became the owner of all his possessions. She used some of the fortune to marry her young sister Anne to a gentleman whom she had loved for a long time. Another portion was used to buy captains' commissions for her brothers. And the rest she kept for herself, for she married an honorable man, whose goodness made her forget the terrible time she had with Blue-Beard.

"Hop O'-My-Thumb" is a popular folk tale—
the following version is by the French storyteller,
Charles Perrault. It also appears in a German
version recorded by Jakob and Wilhelm Grimm a hundred
and fifty years ago. Five stories from their
famous collection follows "Hop O'-My-Thumb."
A word about "Hansel and Gretel."
Like "Tom Thumb" and "Hop O'-My-Thumb,"
it is about the family of a poor woodcutter.
As in "Hop O'-My-Thumb," the father
and mother sadly conclude that,
since they can no longer feed their children,
they had better get rid of them. From that
point on, "Hansel and Gretel" takes
an entirely different course.
The story's appeal became even more widespread
when it was made into an opera by Engelbert Humperdinck
and enjoyed by adults as well as children.

Hop O'-My-Thumb

BY CHARLES PERRAULT ADAPTED BY LOUIS UNTERMEYER.
Illustrated by MAE GERHARD

Once upon a time there was a woodcutter and his wife who had seven children, all boys. They were very poor, and their seven children were a great worry to them, because none of them was yet able to earn his own living. What troubled them most was that the youngest son was very delicate and small. When born he was no larger than a man's thumb; so everybody called him Hop O'-My-Thumb.

There came a famine in the land, and these people, having no food for their children, resolved to get rid of them. One night, when the children were asleep in bed, the woodcutter said to his wife as they sat before the fire, "You see that we can no longer provide for our children. I cannot see them die of hunger. Tomorrow while they are with us, tying up the twigs, we must lose them in the woods."

"Ah!" cried the woodcutter's wife. "How can we!"

"We cannot find even enough food for one!"

Finally, however, she agreed that she could not bear to see the children die of hunger, and so she consented to his plan, and went weeping to bed.

Hop O'-My-Thumb had heard all that had been said. Listening to the voices, he had crept out of bed and had hidden himself under his father's chair, where he could not be seen. After his parents had finished talking he went back to bed. But he did not sleep a wink that night; he kept on thinking what he would have to do. Finally, he decided on a plan.

The next morning he got up early and went to the brookside. There he picked up a lot of white pebbles, filled his pockets with them, and returned home.

Soon after, they entered a thick wood. The woodcutter began to chop wood and, when the children began to gather up the sticks, the mother and father crept off.

When the children found themselves alone, they began to cry. But Hop O'-My-Thumb had dropped the white pebbles all along the way. After letting them cry awhile, he told them to cheer up, for he would lead them back again. So they followed him, and he led them home by the same road by which they came. At first they did not dare to go in, but stood at the door to hear what their parents were saying.

The very moment the woodcutter and his wife arrived home, they received a sum of money which had long been due them for their work. The wife went straight to the butcher's, and got so much meat that when the two had eaten enough, there was still a great deal left, and the woman said, "Alas! where are our poor children? Here is food enough left for them all. I told you it was wrong to leave them in the forest. Perhaps wolves have already eaten them!"

At last she cried so loud that the children heard her, and answered all together, "Here we are! Here we are!"

She ran to the door and, throwing it open, began to embrace them, saying, "How happy I am to see you again, my dear children; how tired and hungry you must be. Come in. You must be starved!"

Their father and mother were well pleased to see them eat, and to hear their voices again.

Everyone talked at once, and there was nothing but joy.

But this happiness did not last. The money was soon spent, and the parents started worrying again. They fell back upon their first plan; but this time they decided to take the children much deeper into the forest.

Hop O'-My-Thumb found out all about it as before. He got up early in the morning to get the pebbles as before; but he found the door locked, so he could not get out. At first he did not know what to do, but they each had a piece of bread for breakfast, and he thought he could mark the road by strewing crumbs along as he had done with the pebbles. So he put his bread into his pocket. Their father and mother led them into the darkest and most tangled part of the forest, and then stole off and left them as before. Hop O'-My-Thumb was not worried. He supposed he could find his way back by the pieces of bread, but he was mistaken; the birds had eaten every crumb.

They were now in great trouble. They wandered deeper into the forest, and were so frightened by the howling of

wolves and the rain and wind that they were afraid to speak. Hop O'-My-Thumb climbed to the top of a tree to see what he could discover. At last, looking everywhere, he spied a light beyond the forest. He came down again, and, after walking toward it with his brothers for some time, they at last came to a house.

They knocked at the door, and a woman, bearing a lamp, appeared. She asked what they wanted. Hop O'-My-Thumb told her they were poor children lost in the forest, and had come to beg a night's rest. The woman, who pitied their forlorn condition, began to cry, and said, "Alas, my children, you have come to the house of an ogre!"

"Oh, madam," he replied, trembling with fear, as did his brothers, "what shall we do? The wolves will certainly eat us up if we stay in the forest, and we would rather take a chance with an ogre. Perhaps your husband, when he sees us, may take pity on us, and spare our lives."

The ogress, hoping she might be able to conceal them, let them come in. While they were warming themselves at a huge fire, before which was a whole sheep roasting for the ogre's supper, they heard three or four heavy blows at the door. It was the ogre, who had come home. The ogress hastily concealed them under the bed, and admitted the ogre, who asked if his supper was ready, and sat down at the table. He began to eat, staring to the right and left, saying: "I smell fresh meat."

"It must be," said the ogress, "that you smell the veal which I am dressing."

"I smell *fresh* meat," roared the ogre. And so saying, he jumped up and went straight to the bed.

"So, madam," said he to his wife, "this is the way you

try to deceive me. I would eat you, too, if you were not so tough. This supply of game comes very well to feed three ogres whom I expect in a few days."

He dragged the children out from under the bed; they fell on their knees, and begged for mercy. But he was an unusually hard-hearted ogre. He sharpened his great knife, and seized one of them, when his wife said, "Why such haste? You have a great deal of meat on hand already."

"You are right," said he, "give them plenty to eat. Fatten them up and put them to bed." The ogress was delighted and gave them a good supper; but they were so frightened they could scarcely eat.

This ogre had seven young daughters. Although they had fine complexions, they had beak-like noses and long sharp teeth. They were not yet wicked, but they were growing up to resemble their father, and they had already bitten several small children. They had gone to bed early, in one large bed, each girl having on her head a golden crown. There was another bed just like it in which the boys were put.

Hop O'-My-Thumb, fearing the ogre would come and kill them during the night, got up after all was quiet, took his brothers' caps and his own, and put them on the heads of the little girls. Then, taking their golden crowns, he put them on the heads of his brothers and himself.

Just as he had expected, the ogre, waking up in the night, was sorry he had put off killing them, and so, taking his great knife, he went upstairs. He groped his way in the dark room, and went to the bed where the little boys lay. He passed his hands over all their heads, and, feeling the crowns, said, "Why, this is strange!"

He then went to the other bed, and, feeling the boys' caps on his daughters' heads, said, "Ah! here you are, my boys!" and in a moment cut the throats of his daughters.

As soon as he was back in bed and snoring, Hop O'-My-Thumb told his brothers to get up and dress themselves and follow him. They went down softly into the garden and jumped over the wall. They ran all the rest of the night, trembling and fearful, not knowing where they were.

In the morning the ogre told his wife to go up and dress the little boys. She was much surprised at his kindness, thinking he meant her to put on their clothes. She went to the room, and, seeing her seven daughters bathed in blood, fainted at the sight. The ogre, getting impatient at his wife's delay, went up himself, and was astonished at the frightful sight.

"Ah!" said he, "what have I done? The wretches shall pay for this!"

He then revived his wife and told her to bring his seven-league boots, so that he might pursue the children. He set out, and, after going in every direction, at last came into the same road where the children were walking, not a hundred rods from their father's house. They saw the ogre striding over the country, and, finding a hollow rock, crept behind it, and waited for him to pass. Being very tired from his long walk (for the boots were quite hard to wear), the ogre happened to sit down on the very rock behind which the little boys were concealed. Weary with fatigue, he went to sleep. Hop O'-My-Thumb, taking courage, told his brothers to run home while the ogre was snoring, which they did.

Then Hop O'-My-Thumb crept out, went quietly to the ogre, softly pulled off his seven-league boots, and put them on himself. They were very clumsy, but, since they were magic boots, they had the power of growing large or small to fit the foot of the wearer. He went straight to the ogre's house and told his wife that the ogre had been seized by a band of robbers who had threatened his life, unless he should give up all his gold and silver. "He told me to wear these boots, and to come for all his treasures."

The ogress, terribly alarmed, gave him the key to all the ogre's wealth. Hop O'-My-Thumb took as much as he could carry, and went straight home, where he was received with great joy, and they lived in ease ever after.

Hansel and Gretel

BY JAKOB AND WILHELM GRIMM
Illustrated by ELOISE WILKIN

Near a great forest there lived a poor woodcutter and his wife, and his two children. The boy's name was Hansel and the girl's, Gretel. They had very little to bite or to sup, and once, when there was much want in the land, the man could not even earn the daily bread.

As he lay in bed one night thinking of this, and turning and tossing, he sighed heavily, and said to his wife, who was the children's stepmother,

"What will become of us? We cannot even feed our children; there is nothing left for ourselves."

"I will tell you what, husband," answered the wife; "we will take the children early in the morning into the forest, where it is thickest; we will make them a fire, and we will give each of them a piece of bread, then we will go to our work and leave them alone; they will never find the way home again, and we shall be quit of them."

"No, wife," said the man, "I cannot do that; I cannot find it in my heart to take my children into the forest and to leave them there alone; the wild animals would soon come and devour them."

"Oh you fool," said she, "then we will all four starve; you had better get the coffins ready," and she left him no peace until he consented.

The two children had not been able to sleep for hunger, and had heard what their stepmother had said to their father. Gretel wept bitterly, and said to Hansel,

"It is all over with us."

"Do be quiet, Gretel," said Hansel, "and do not fret; I will manage something." When the parents had gone to sleep, Hansel got up, put on his little coat, opened the back door, and slipped out. The moon was shining brightly, and the white pebbles that lay in front of the house glistened like pieces of silver. Hansel stooped and filled the little pocket of his coat as full as it would hold. Then he went back again, and said to Gretel,

"Be easy, dear little sister, and go to sleep quietly; God will not forsake us," and laid himself down again in his bed.

When the day was breaking, and before the sun had risen, the wife came and awakened the two children, saying,

"Get up, you lazy bones! We are going into the forest to cut wood."

Then she gave each of them a piece of bread, and said,

"That is for dinner, and you must not eat it before then, for you will get no more."

Gretel carried the bread under her apron, for Hansel had his pockets full of pebbles. Then they set off all together on their way to the forest. When they had gone a little way Hansel stood still and looked back toward the house, and this he did again and again, till his father said to him,

"Hansel, what are you looking at? Take care not to forget your legs."

"Oh Father," said Hansel, "I am looking at my little white kitten, who is sitting up on the roof to bid me good-bye."

"You foolish boy," said the woman, "that is not your kitten, but the sunshine on the chimney pot."

Of course Hansel had not been looking at his kitten, but had been taking every now and then a pebble from his pocket and dropping it on the road.

When they reached the middle of the forest the father told the children to collect wood to make a fire to keep them warm; and Hansel and

Gretel gathered brushwood enough for a little mountain; and it was set on fire, and when the flame was burning quite high the wife said,

"Now lie down by the fire and rest yourselves, you children, and we will go and cut wood; and when we are ready we will come and fetch you."

So Hansel and Gretel sat by the fire, and at noon they each ate their pieces of bread. They thought their father was in the wood all the time, as they seemed to hear the strokes of the ax, but really it was only a dry branch hanging to a withered tree that the wind moved to and fro.

So when they had stayed there a long time their eyelids closed with weariness, and they fell fast asleep. When at last they woke it was night, and Gretel began to cry, and said,

"How shall we ever get out of this wood?" But Hansel comforted her, saying,

"Wait a little while longer, until the moon rises, and then we can easily find the way home."

And when the full moon came up, Hansel took his little sister by the hand, and followed the way where the pebbles shone like silver, and

showed them the road. They walked on the whole night through, and at the break of day they came to their father's house. They knocked at the door, and when their stepmother opened it and saw that it was Hansel and Gretel she said,

"You naughty children, why did you sleep so long in the wood? We thought you were never coming home again!"

But the father was glad, for it had gone to his heart to leave them both in the woods alone.

Not very long after that there was again great scarcity in those parts, and the children heard their stepmother say to their father,

"Everything is finished up; we have only half a loaf, and after that the tale comes to an end. The children must be off; we will take them farther into the wood this time, so that they shall not be able to find the way back again. There is no other way to manage."

The man felt sad at heart, and he thought,

"It would be better to share one's last morsel with one's children."

But the wife would listen to nothing that he said, but scolded and reproached him.

But the children were not asleep, and had heard all the talk. When the parents had gone to sleep, Hansel got up to go out and get more pebbles as he did before, but the stepmother had locked the door, and Hansel could not get out; but he comforted his little sister, and said,

"Don't cry, Gretel, and go to sleep quietly, and God will help us."

Early the next morning the wife came and pulled the children out of bed. She gave them each a little piece of bread—less than before; and on the way to the wood Hansel crumbled the bread in his pocket, and often stopped to throw a crumb on the ground.

"Hansel, what are you stopping behind and staring for?" said the father.

"I am looking at my little pigeon sitting on the roof, to say good-bye to me," answered Hansel.

54

"You foolish boy," said the wife, "that is no pigeon, but the morning sun shining on the chimney pots."

Hansel went on as before, and strewed bread crumbs all along the road.

The woman led the children far into the wood, where they had never been before in all their lives. And again there was a large fire made, and the stepmother said,

"Sit still there, you children, and when you are tired you can go to sleep; we are going into the forest to cut wood, and in the evening, when we are ready to go home, we will come and fetch you."

So when noon came Gretel shared her bread with Hansel, who had strewed his along the road.

Then they went to sleep, and the evening passed, and no one came for the poor children. When they awoke it was dark night, and Hansel comforted his little sister, and said,

"Wait a little, Gretel, until the moon gets up; then we shall be able to see our way home by the crumbs of bread that I have scattered along the road."

So when the moon rose they got up, but they could find no crumbs of bread, for the birds of the woods and of the fields had come and picked them up. Hansel thought they might find the way all the same, but they could not.

They went on all that night, and the next day from the morning until the evening, but they could not find the way out of the wood, and they were very hungry, for they had nothing to eat but the few berries they could pick up. And when they were so tired that they could no longer drag themselves along, they lay down under a tree and fell asleep.

It was now the third morning since they had left their father's house. They were always trying to get back to it, but instead of that they only found themselves farther in the wood, and if help had not soon come they would have been starved. About noon they saw a pretty snow-white bird sitting on a bough, and singing so sweetly that they stopped to listen. And when he had finished, the bird spread his wings and flew before them, and they followed after him until they came to a little house, and the bird perched on the roof, and when they came nearer they saw that the house was built of gingerbread, and roofed with cakes; and the window was of transparent sugar.

"We will have some of this," said Hansel, "and make a fine meal. I will eat a piece of the roof, Gretel, and you can have some of the window—that will taste sweet."

So Hansel reached up and broke off a bit of the roof, just to see how it tasted, and Gretel stood by the window and gnawed at it. Then they heard a thin voice call out from inside,

"*Nibble, nibble, like a mouse,*
Who is nibbling at my house?"

And the children answered,
    "Never mind,
      It is the wind."

And they went on eating, never disturbing themselves. Hansel, who found that the roof tasted very nice, took down a great piece of it, and Gretel pulled out a large round windowpane, and sat her down and began upon it. Then the door opened, and an aged woman came out, leaning upon a crutch. Hansel and Gretel felt very frightened, and let fall what they had in their hands. The old woman, however, nodded her head, and said,

"Ah, my dear children, how come you here? You must come indoors and stay with me. You will be no trouble."

So she took them each by the hand, and led them into her little house. And there they found a good meal laid out, of milk and pancakes, with sugar, apples, and nuts. After that she showed them two little white beds, and Hansel and Gretel laid themselves down on them, and thought they were in heaven.

The old woman, although her behavior was so kind, was a wicked witch, who lay in wait for children, and had built the little house on purpose to entice them. When they were once inside she used to kill them, cook them, and eat them, and then it was a feast-day with her. The witch's eyes were red, and she could not see very far, but she had

a keen scent, like the beasts, and knew very well when human crea-tures were near. When she knew that Hansel and Gretel were coming, she gave a spiteful laugh, and said triumphantly,

"I have them, and they shall not escape me!"

Early in the morning, before the children were awake, she got up to look at them, and as they lay sleeping so peacefully with round rosy cheeks, she said to herself,

"What a fine feast I shall have!"

She grasped Hansel with her withered hand, and led him into a little stable, and shut him up behind a grating; and call and scream as he might, it was no good. Then she went back to Gretel and shook her, crying,

"Get up, lazy bones! Fetch water, and cook something nice for your brother; he is outside in the stable, and must be fattened up. And when he is fat enough, I will eat him."

Gretel began to weep bitterly, but it was of no use. She had to do what the wicked witch bade her.

And so the best kind of victuals was cooked for poor Hansel, while Gretel got nothing but crab shells. Each morning the old woman visited the little stable, and cried,

"Hansel, stretch out your finger, that I may tell if you will soon be fat enough."

Hansel, however, held out a little bone, and the old woman, who had weak eyes, could not see what it was, and supposing it to be Hansel's finger, wondered very much that it was not getting fatter. When four weeks had passed and Hansel seemed to remain so thin, she lost pa-tience and could wait no longer.

"Now then, Gretel," cried she to the little girl, "be quick and draw water. Be Hansel fat or be he lean, tomorrow I must kill and cook him."

Oh, what a grief for the poor little sister to have to fetch water, and how the tears flowed down over her cheeks!

"Dear God, pray help us!" cried she. "If we had been devoured by wild beasts in the wood, at least we should have died together."

"Spare me your lamentations," said the old woman. "They are of no avail."

Early next morning Gretel had to get up, make the fire, and fill the kettle.

"First we will do the baking," said the old woman. "I have heated the oven already, and kneaded the dough."

She pushed poor Gretel towards the oven, out of which the flames were already shining.

"Creep in," said the witch, "and see if it is properly hot so that the bread may be baked."

And Gretel once in, she meant to shut the door upon her and let her be baked, and then she would have eaten her. But Gretel perceived her intention, and said,

"I don't know how to do it. How shall I get in?"

"Stupid goose," said the old woman, "the opening is big enough, do you see? I could get in myself!" and she stooped down and put her head in the oven's mouth. Then Gretel gave her a push, so that she went in farther, and she shut the iron door upon her, and put up the bar. Oh, how frightfully she howled! But Gretel ran away, and left her in the

oven. Then Gretel went straight to Hansel, opened the stable door and cried,

"Hansel, we are free! The old witch is dead!"

Then out flew Hansel like a bird from its cage as soon as the door is opened. How rejoiced they both were! How they fell each on the other's neck! And danced about, and kissed each other! And as they had nothing more to fear, they went over all the old witch's house, and in every corner there stood chests of pearls and precious stones.

"This is something better than pebbles," said Hansel, as he filled his pockets. And Gretel, thinking she also would like to carry something home with her, filled her apron full.

"Now, away we go," said Hansel, "if we only can get out of the witch's wood!"

When they had journeyed a few hours they came to a great piece of water.

"We can never get across this," said Hansel. "I see no stepping-stones and no bridge."

"And there is no boat either," said Gretel. "But here comes a white duck; if I ask her, she will help us over." So she cried,

> *"Duck, duck, here we stand,*
> *Hansel and Gretel on the land,*
> *Stepping-stones and bridge we lack,*
> *Carry us over on your nice white back."*

And the duck came accordingly, and Hansel got upon her and told his sister to come too.

"No," answered Gretel, "that would be too hard upon the duck; we can go separately, one after the other."

And that was how it was managed, and after that they went on happily, until they came to the wood, and the way grew more and more familiar, till at last they saw in the distance their father's house. Then they ran till they came up to it, rushed in at the door, and fell on their

father's neck. The man had not had a quiet hour since he left his children in the wood; but his wife was dead. And when Gretel opened her apron, the pearls and precious stones were scattered all over the room, and Hansel took one handful after another out of his pocket. Then was all care at an end, and they lived in great joy together.

68

Tom Thumb

BY JAKOB AND WILHELM GRIMM
Illustrated by WILLIAM DUGAN

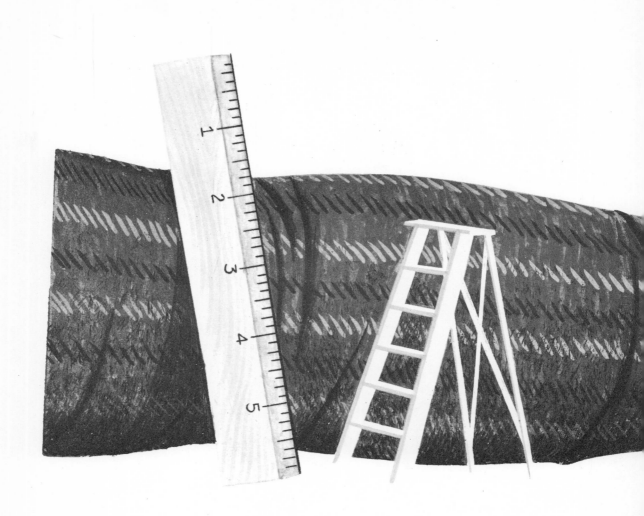

There was once a poor woodman sitting by the fire in his cottage, and his wife sat by his side spinning. "How lonely it is," said he, "for you and me to sit here by ourselves without any children to play about and amuse us, while other people seem so happy and merry with their children!" "What you say is very true," said the wife, sighing and turning round her wheel; "how happy should I be if I had but one child! and if it were ever so small, and, if it were no bigger than my thumb, I should be very happy, and love it dearly."

70

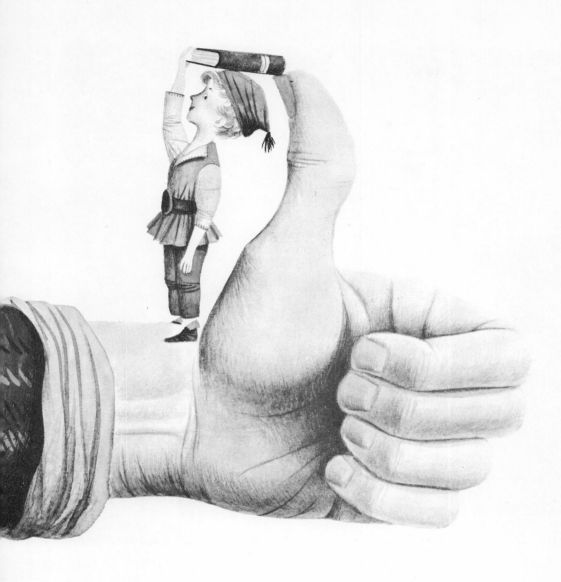

Now it came to pass that this good woman's wish was fulfilled just as she desired; for, some time afterwards, she had a little boy who was quite healthy and strong but not much bigger than my thumb. So they said, "Well, we cannot say we have not got what we wished for, and, little as he is, we still love him dearly;" and they called him Tom Thumb.

They gave him plenty of food, yet he never grew bigger, but remained just the same size as when he was born. Still his eyes were sharp and sparkling, and he soon showed himself to be a clever fellow.

One day, as the woodman was getting ready to go into the wood to cut fuel, he said, "I wish I had someone to bring the cart after me, for I want to make haste." "O father!" cried Tom, "I will take care of that; the cart shall be in the wood by the time you want it." Then the woodman laughed, and said, "How can that be? You cannot reach up to the donkey's bridle." "Never mind that, father," said Tom. "If my mother will only harness the donkey, I will get into his ear, and tell him which way to go." "Well," said the father, "we will try for once."

When the time came, the mother harnessed the donkey to the cart, and put Tom into his ear; and as he sat there, the little man told the beast how to go, crying out "Go on!" and "Stop!" as he wanted; so the donkey went on just as if the woodman had driven it himself into the

wood. It happened that, as the donkey was going a little too fast, and Tom was calling out "Gently! gently!" two strangers came up. "What an odd thing that is!" said one. "There is a cart going along, and I hear a carter talking to the donkey, but can see no one." "That is strange," said the other. "Let us follow the cart and see where it goes."

So they went on into the wood till at last they came to the place where the woodman was. Then Tom Thumb, seeing his father, cried out, "See, father, here I am, with the cart, all right and safe; now take me down." So his father took hold of the donkey with one hand, and with the other took his son out of the ear; then he put him down upon a straw, where he sat as merry as you please.

The two strangers were all this time looking on, and did not know

what to say for wonder. At last one took the other aside, and said, "That little urchin will make our fortune if we can get him, and carry him about from town to town as a show; we must buy him."

So they went to the woodman and asked him what he would take for the little man. "He will be better off," said they, "with us than with you." "I won't sell him at all," said the father. "My own flesh and blood is dearer to me than all the silver and gold in the world." But Tom, hearing of the bargain they wanted to make, crept up his father's coat to his shoulder, and whispered in his ear, "Take the money, father, and let them have me, I'll soon come back to you."

So the woodman at last agreed to sell Tom to the strangers for a large piece of gold. "Where do you like to sit?" said one of them. "Oh! put me on the rim of your hat, that will be a nice gallery for me; I can walk about there, and see the country as we go along." So they did as he wished; and when Tom had taken leave of his father, they took him away with them.

They journeyed on till it began to be dusky, and then the little man said, "Let me get down, I'm tired." So the man took off his hat and set him down on a clod of earth in a ploughed field by the side of the road. But Tom ran about amongst the furrows, and at last slipped into an old mouse-hole. "Good-night, masters," said he, "I'm off! Mind and

look sharp after me the next time." They ran directly to the place, and and poked the ends of their sticks into the mouse-hole, but all in vain; Tom only crawled farther and farther in, and last it became quite dark, so that they were obliged to go their way without their prize, as sulky as you please.

When Tom found they were gone, he came out of his hiding-place. "What dangerous walking it is," said he, "in this ploughed field! If I were to fall from one of these great clods, I should certainly break my neck." At last, by good luck, he found a large empty snail-shell. "This is lucky," said he. "I can sleep here very well," and in he crept. Just as he was falling asleep he heard two men passing, and one said to the other, "How shall we manage to steal that rich parson's silver and gold?"

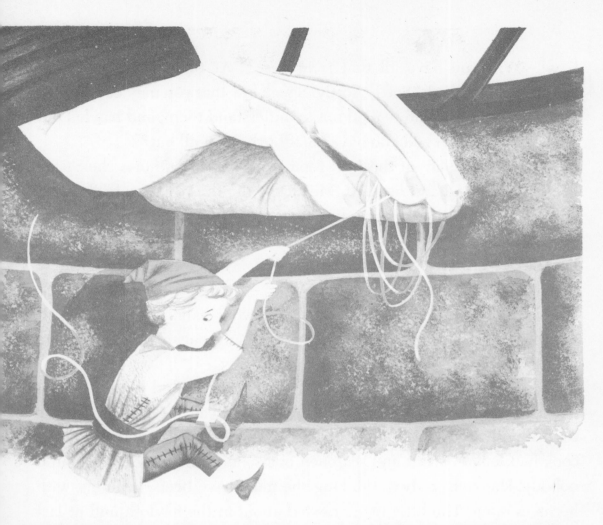

"I'll tell you!" cried Tom. "What noise was that?" said the thief, frightened. "I am sure I heard someone speak."

They stood still listening, and Tom said, "Take me with you, and I'll soon show you how to get the parson's money." "But where are you?" said they. "Look about on the ground," answered he, "and listen where the sound comes from." At last the thieves found him out, and lifted him up in their hands. "You little urchin!" said they. "What can you do for us?" "Why, I can get between the iron window-bars of the parson's house and throw you out whatever you want." "That's a good thought," said the thieves; "come along, we shall see what you can do."

When they came to the parson's house, Tom slipped through the window-bars into the room, and then called out as loud as he could bawl, "Will you have all that is in here?" At this the thieves were frightened, and said, "Softly, softly! Speak low that you may not awaken anybody." But Tom pretended not to understand them, and bawled out again, "How much will you have? Shall I throw it all out?"

Now the cook lay in the next room, and hearing a noise she raised herself in her bed and listened. Meantime the thieves were frightened, and ran off to a little distance; but at last they plucked up courage, and said, "The little urchin is only trying to make fools of us." So they came back and whispered softly to him, saying, "Now let us have no more of your jokes, but throw out some of the money." Then Tom called out as loud as he could, "Very well: hold your hands, here it comes!" The cook heard this quite plain, so she sprang out of bed and ran to open the door.

The thieves ran off as if a wolf were at their tails; and the maid, having groped about and found nothing, went away for a light. By the time she returned, Tom had slipped off into the barn; and when the cook had looked about and searched every hole and corner, and found nobody, she went to bed, thinking she must have been dreaming with her eyes open. The little man crawled about in the hayloft, and at last found a glorious place to finish his night's rest in; so he laid himself down, meaning to sleep till daylight, and then find his way home to his father and mother.

But, alas! how cruelly was he disappointed! what crosses and sorrows happen in this world! The cook got up early before daybreak to feed the cows: she went straight to the hay-loft, and carried away a large bundle of hay with the little man in the middle of it fast asleep. He still, however, slept on, and did not awake till he found himself in the mouth of the cow, who had taken him up with a mouthful of hay.

"Lack-a-day!" said he. "How did I manage to tumble into the mill?" But he soon found out where he really was, and was obliged to have all his wits about him in order that he might not get between the cow's teeth, and so be crushed to death. At last down he went into her stomach. "It is rather dark here," said he; "they forgot to build windows in this room to let the sun in: a candle would be no bad thing."

Though he made the best of his bad luck, he did not like his quarters at all; and the worst of it was that more and more hay was always coming down, and the space in which he was became smaller and smaller. At last he cried out as loud as he could, "Don't bring me any more hay! Don't bring me any more hay!" The maid happened to be just then milking the cow, and hearing someone speak and seeing nobody, and yet being quite sure it was the same voice that she had heard in the night, she was so frightened that she fell off her stool and overset the milkpail. She ran off as fast as she could to her master the parson, and said, "Sir, sir, the cow is talking!" But the parson said, "Woman, thou art surely mad!" However, he went with her into the cowhouse to see what was the matter.

Scarcely had they set their foot on the threshold when Tom called out, "Don't bring me any more hay!" Then the parson himself was frightened; and thinking the cow was surely bewitched, ordered that she should be killed directly. So the cow was killed, and the stomach, in which Tom lay, was thrown out upon a dunghill.

Tom soon set himself to work to get out, which was not a very easy task; but at last, just as he had made room to get his head out, a new misfortune befell him; a hungry wolf sprang out, and swallowed the whole stomach, with Tom in it, at a single gulp, and ran away. Tom, however, was not disheartened. Thinking the wolf would not dislike having some chat with him as he was going along, he called out, "My good friend, I can show you a famous treat." "Where's that?" said the wolf. "In such and such a house," said Tom, describing his father's house; "you can crawl through the drain into the kitchen, and there you will find cakes, ham, beef, and everything your heart can desire." The wolf did not want to be asked twice; so that very night he went to the house

and crawled through the drain into the kitchen, and ate and drank there to his heart's content.

As soon as he was satisfied, he wanted to get away; but he had eaten so much that he could not get out the same way as he came in. This was just what Tom had reckoned upon; and he now began to set up a great shout, making all the noise he could. "Will you be quiet?" said the wolf. "You'll awaken everybody in the house." "What's that to me?" said the little man: "you have had a frolic; now I've a mind to be merry myself;" and he began again singing and shouting as loud as he could.

The woodman and his wife, being awakened by the noise, peeped through a crack in the door. When they saw that the wolf was there, you may well suppose that they were terribly frightened; and the wood-

man ran for his axe, and gave his wife a scythe. "Now do you stay behind," said the woodman, "and when I have knocked him on the head, do you rip up his belly for him with the scythe."

Tom heard all this, and said, "Father, father! I am here; the wolf has swallowed me;" and his father said, "Heaven be praised! we have found our dear child again;" and he told his wife not to use the scythe, for fear she should hurt him. Then he aimed a great blow, and struck the wolf on the head, and killed him on the spot; and when he was dead they cut open his body and set Tom free.

"Ah!" said the father, "what fears we have had for you!" "Yes, father," answered he, "I have traveled all over the world since we parted, in one way or other; and now I am very glad to get fresh air again." "Why, where have you been?" said his father. "I have been in a mouse hole, in a snail shell, down a cow's throat, and in the wolf's belly; and yet here I am again safe and sound." "Well," said they, "we will not sell you again for all the riches in the world." So they hugged and kissed their dear little son, and gave him plenty to eat and drink. And that night, the townspeople gathered to hear the wondrous adventures of Tom Thumb.

84

Snow-White and Rose-Red

BY JAKOB AND WILHELM GRIMM
Illustrated by GORDON LAITE

THERE was once a poor widow who lived in a lonely cottage. In front of the cottage was a garden wherein stood two rose trees, one of which bore white and the other red roses. She had two children who were like the two rose trees, and one was called Snow-White, and the other Rose-Red. They were as good and happy, as busy and cheerful as ever two children in the world were, only Snow-White was

85

more quiet and gentle than Rose-Red. Rose-Red liked better to run about in the meadows and fields seeking flowers and catching butterflies; but Snow-White sat at home with her mother, and helped her with her house-work, or read to her when there was nothing to do.

their mother would add, "What one has she must share with the other."

They often ran about the forest alone and gathered red berries, and no beasts did them any harm, but came close to them trustfully. The little hare would eat a cabbage leaf out of their hands, the roe

The two children were so fond of each other that they always held each other by the hand when they went out together, and when Snow-White said, "We will not leave each other," Rose-Red answered. "Never so long as we live," and

grazed by their side, the stag leapt merrily by them, and the birds sat still upon the boughs, and sang whatever they knew.

No mishap overtook them; if they had stayed too late in the forest, and night came on, they laid themselves down near one another upon the moss, and slept until morning came, and their mother knew this and had no distress on their account.

Once when they had spent the night in the wood and the dawn had roused them, they saw a beautiful child in a shining white dress sitting near their bed. He got up and looked quite kindly at them, but said nothing and went away into the forest. And when they looked round they found that they had been sleeping quite close to a precipice, and would certainly have fallen into it if they had gone only a few paces further. And their mother told them that it must have been the angel who watches over good children.

Snow-White and Rose-Red kept their mother's little cottage so neat that it was a pleasure to look inside it. In the summer Rose-Red took care of the house, and every morning laid a wreath of flowers by her mother's bed before she awoke, in which was a rose from each tree. In the winter Snow-White lit the fire and hung the kettle on its iron hook above the hearth. The kettle was of copper and shone like gold, so brightly was it polished. In the evening, when the snowflakes fell, the mother said, "Go, Snow-White, and bolt the door," and then they sat round the hearth, and the mother took her spectacles and read aloud out of a large book, and the two girls listened as they sat and spun. And close by them lay a lamb upon the floor, and behind them upon a perch sat a white dove with its head hidden beneath its wings.

One evening, as they were thus sitting comfortably together, someone knocked at the door as if he wished to be let in. The mother said, "Quick, Rose-Red, open the door; it must be a traveler who is seeking shelter." Rose-Red went and pushed back the bolt, thinking that it was a poor man, but it was not; it was a bear that stretched his broad, black head within the door.

Rose-Red screamed and sprang back, the lamb bleated, the dove fluttered, and Snow-White hid herself behind her mother's bed. But the bear began to speak and said, "Do not be afraid, I will do you no harm! I am half-frozen, and only want to warm myself a little beside you."

"Poor bear," said the mother, "lie down by the fire, only take care that you do not burn your coat." Then she cried, "Snow-White, Rose-Red, come out, the bear will do you no harm, he means well." So they both came out, and by-and-by the lamb and dove came nearer, and were not afraid of him.

The bear said, "Here, children, knock the snow out of my coat a little." So they brought the broom and swept the bear's hide clean; and he stretched himself by the fire and growled contentedly and comfortably. It was not long before they grew quite at home, and played tricks with their clumsy guest. They tugged his hair with their hands, put their feet upon his back and rolled him about, or they took a hazel-switch and beat him, and when he growled they laughed. But the bear took it all in good part, only when they were too rough he called out, "Leave me alive, children,

Snowy-White, Rosy-Red,
Will you beat your lover dead?"

When it was bed time, and the others went to bed, the mother said to the bear, "You can lie there by the hearth, and then you will be safe from the cold and the bad weather." As soon as day dawned the two children let him out, and he trotted across the snow into the forest.

Henceforth the bear came every evening at the same time, laid himself down by the hearth, and let the children amuse themselves with him as much as they liked; and they got so used to him that the doors were never fastened until their black friend had arrived.

When spring had come and all outside was green, the bear said one morning to Snow-White, "Now I must go away, and cannot come back for the whole summer."

"Where are you going, then, dear bear?" asked Snow-White.

"I must go into the forest and guard my treasures from the wicked dwarfs. In the winter, when the earth is frozen hard, they are obliged to stay below and cannot work their way through; but now, when the sun has thawed and warmed the earth, they break through it, and come out to pry and steal. And what once gets into their hands, and in their caves, does not easily see daylight again."

Snow-White was quite sorry for his going away, and as she unbolted the door for him, and the bear was hurrying out, he caught against the bolt and a piece of his hairy coat was torn off, and it seemed to Snow-White as if she had seen gold shining through it, but she was not sure about it. The bear ran away quickly, and was soon out of sight behind the trees.

A short time afterwards the mother sent her children into the forest to get fire-wood. There they found a big tree

which lay felled on the ground, and close by the trunk something was jumping backwards and forwards in the grass, but they could not make out what it was. When they came nearer they saw a dwarf with an old withered face and a snow-white beard a yard long. The end of the beard was caught in a crevice of the tree, and the little fellow was jumping backwards and forwards like a dog tied to a rope, and did not know what to do.

He glared at the girls with his fiery red eyes and cried, "Why do you stand there? Can you not come here and help me?"

"What are you about there, little man?" asked Rose-Red.

"You stupid, prying goose!" answered the dwarf; "I was going to split the tree to get a little wood for cooking. The little bit of food that one of us wants gets burnt up directly with thick logs; we do not swallow so much as you coarse, greedy folk. I had just driven the wedge safely in, and everything was going as I wished; but the wretched wood was too smooth and suddenly sprang asunder, and the tree closed so quickly that I could not pull out my beautiful white beard. So now it is tight in and I cannot get away, and the silly, sleek, milk-faced things laugh! Ugh! how odious you are!"

The children tried very hard, but they

89

could not pull the beard out, it was caught too fast. "I will run and fetch someone," said Rose-Red.

"You senseless goose!" snarled the dwarf; "why should you fetch someone? You are already two too many for me; can you not think of something better?"

"Don't be impatient," said Snow-White, "I will help you," and she pulled her scissors out of her pocket, and cut off the end of the beard.

As soon as the dwarf felt himself free he laid hold of a bag which lay amongst the roots of the tree, and which was full of gold, and lifted it up, grumbling to himself, "Uncouth people, to cut off a piece of my fine beard. Bad luck to you!" and then he swung the bag upon his back, and went off without even once looking at the children.

Some time after that Snow-White and

Rose-Red went to catch a dish of fish. As they came near the brook they saw something like a large grasshopper jumping towards the water, as if it were going to leap in. They ran to it and found it was the dwarf. "Where are you going?" said Rose-Red; "you surely don't want to go into the water?"

"I am not such a fool!" cried the dwarf; "don't you see that the accursed fish wants to pull me in?" The little man had been sitting there fishing, and unluckily the wind had twisted his beard with the fishing-line. Just then a big fish bit, and the feeble creature had not strength to pull it out. The fish kept the upper hand and pulled the dwarf towards him. He held on to all the reeds and rushes, but it was of little good, he was forced to follow the movements of the fish, and was in urgent danger of being dragged into the water.

The girls came just in time; they held him fast and tried to free his beard from the line, but all in vain; beard and line were entangled fast together. Nothing was left but to bring out the scissors and cut the beard, whereby a small part of it was lost. When the dwarf saw that, he screamed out, "Is that civil, you toad-stool, to disfigure one's face? Was it not enough to clip off the end of my beard? Now you have cut off the best part of it. I cannot let myself be seen by my people. I wish you had been made to run the soles off your shoes!" Then he took out a sack of pearls which lay in the rushes, and without saying a word more he dragged it away and disappeared behind a stone.

It happened that soon afterwards the mother sent the two children to the town to buy needles and thread, and laces and ribbons. The road led them across a heath upon which huge pieces of rock lay strewn here and there. Now they noticed a large bird hovering in the air, flying slowly round and round above them; it sank lower and lower, and at last settled near a rock not far off. Directly afterwards they heard a loud, piteous cry. They ran up and saw with horror that the eagle had seized their old acquaintance the dwarf, and was going to carry him off.

The children, full of pity, at once took tight hold of the little man, and pulled against the eagle so long that at last he let his booty go. As soon as the dwarf had recovered from his first fright he cried with his shrill voice, "Could you not have done it more carefully! You dragged at my brown coat so that it is all torn and full of holes, you helpless clumsy creatures!" Then he took up a sack full of precious stones, and slipped away again under the rock into his hole. The girls, who by this time were used to his thanklessness, went on their way and did their business in the town.

As they crossed the heath again on their way home they surprised the dwarf,

who had emptied out his bag of precious
stones in a clean spot, and had not
thought that anyone would come there
so late. The evening sun shone upon the
brilliant stones; they glittered and sparkled with all colors so beautifully that
the children stood still and looked at
them. "Why do you stand gaping there?"
cried the dwarf, and his ashen-gray face
became copper-red with rage. He was
going on with his bad words when a loud
growling was heard, and a black bear

came trotting towards them out of the
forest. The dwarf sprang up in a fright,
but he could not get to his cave, for the
bear was already close. Then in the dread
of his heart he cried, "Dear Mr. Bear,
spare me, I will give you all my treasures;
look, the beautiful jewels lying there!
Grant me my life; what do you want with
such a slender little fellow as I? You
would not feel me between your teeth.
Come, take these two wicked girls, they
are tender morsels for you, fat as young

quails. For mercy's sake eat them!" The bear took no heed of his words, but gave the wicked creature a single blow with his paw, and he did not move again.

The girls had run away, but the bear called to them, "Snow-White and Rose-Red, do not be afraid; wait, I will come with you." Then they knew his voice and waited, and when he came up to them suddenly his bearskin fell off, and he stood there a handsome man, clothed all in gold. "I am a King's son," he said, "and I was bewitched by that wicked dwarf, who had stolen my treasures. I have had to run about the forest as a savage bear until I was freed by his death. Now he has got his well-deserved punishment."

Snow-White was married to him, and Rose-Red to his brother, and they divided between them the great treasure which the dwarf had gathered together in his cave. The old mother lived peacefully and happily with her children for many years. She took the two rose trees with her, and they stood before her window, and every year bore the most beautiful roses, white and red.

Rapunzel

BY JAKOB AND WILHELM GRIMM
Illustrated by GORDON LAITE

THERE once lived a man and his wife, who had long wished for a child, but in vain. Now there was at the back of their house a little window which overlooked a beautiful garden full of the finest vegetables and flowers; but there was a high wall round it, and no one ventured into it, for it belonged to a witch of great might, who was feared by all the world. One day that the wife was standing at the window, and looking into the garden, she saw a bed filled with the finest rampion; and it looked so fresh and green that she began to wish for some; and at length she longed for it greatly. This went on for days, and as she knew she could not get the rampion, her desire grew greater and greater, until she pined away, and grew pale and miserable. Then her husband was uneasy, and asked,

"What is the matter, dear wife?"

"Oh," answered she, "I shall die unless I can have some of that rampion to eat that grows in the garden at the back of

our house." The man, who loved her very much, thought to himself,

"Rather than lose my wife I will get some rampion, cost what it will."

So in the twilight he climbed over the wall into the witch's garden, hastily plucked a handful of rampion and brought it to his wife. She made a salad of it at once; and ate of it to her heart's content. But she liked it so much, and it tasted so good, that the next day she longed for it thrice as much as she had done before. If she was to have any rest the man must climb over the wall once more. So he went in the twilight again; and as he was climbing back, he saw, all at once, the witch standing before him, and was terribly frightened, as she cried, with angry eyes,

"How dare you climb over into my garden like a thief, and steal my rampion! You shall suffer for this!"

"Oh," answered he, "be merciful rather than just, I have only done it through necessity; for my wife saw your rampion out of the window, and became possessed with so great a longing that she would have died if she could not have had some." Then the witch said,

"If it is all as you say you may have as much rampion as you like, on one condition—the child that your wife will shortly bring into the world must be given to me. And I will care for it like a mother."

In his distress of mind the man promised everything; and when the time came when the child was born the witch appeared, and giving the child the name of Rapunzel (which is the same as rampion), she took it away with her.

Rapunzel was the most beautiful child in the world. When she was twelve years old the witch shut her up in a tower in the midst of a wood, and it had neither steps nor door, only a small window high above. When the witch wished to be let in, she would stand below and cry,

> "*Rapunzel, Rapunzel,*
> *Let down your golden hair.*"

Rapunzel had beautiful long hair that shone like gold. When she heard the voice of the witch she would undo the fastening of the upper window, unbind the plaits of her hair, and let it down twenty ells below, and the witch would climb up by it.

After they had lived thus a few years it happened that as the King's son was riding through the wood, he came to the tower; and as he drew near he heard a voice singing so sweetly that he stood still and listened. It was Rapunzel in her loneliness trying to pass away the time with sweet songs. The King's son wished to go in to her, and sought to find a door in the tower, but there was none. So he rode home, but the song had entered into his heart, and every day he went into the wood and listened to it. Once, as he was standing there under a tree, he saw the witch come up, and listened while she called out,

"*Rapunzel, Rapunzel,*
Let down your golden hair."

Then he saw how Rapunzel let down her long tresses, and how the witch climbed up by them and went in to her, and he said to himself,

"Since that is the ladder I will climb it, and try my luck." And the next day, as soon as it began to grow dusk, he went to the tower and cried,

"*Rapunzel, Rapunzel,*
Let down your golden hair."

And she let down her hair, and the King's son climbed up by it.

Rapunzel was greatly terrified when she saw that a man had come in, for she had never seen one before. But the King's son began speaking so kindly to her, and told how her singing had entered into his heart, so that he could have no peace until he had seen her. Then Rapunzel forgot her terror, and when he asked her to take him for her husband, and she saw that he was young and beautiful, she thought to herself,

"I certainly like him much better than old mother Gothel," and she put her hand into his hand, saying,

"I would willingly go with thee, but I do not know how I shall get out. When thou comest, bring each time a silken rope, and I will make a ladder, and when it is quite ready I will get down by it out of the tower, and thou shalt take me away on thy horse." They agreed that he should come to her every evening, as the old woman came in the day-time. So the witch knew nothing of all this until once Rapunzel said to her unwittingly,

"Mother Gothel, how is it that you climb up here so slowly, and the King's son is with me in a moment?"

"O wicked child," cried the witch, "what is this I hear! I thought I had hidden thee from all the world, and thou hast betrayed me!"

In her anger she seized Rapunzel by her beautiful hair, struck her several times with her left hand, and then grasping a pair of shears in her right—snip, snap—the beautiful braids lay on the ground. And she was so hard-hearted that she took Rapunzel and put her in a lonely desert place, to live in loneliness and misery.

The same day on which she took Rapunzel away she went back to the tower in the evening and made fast the severed braid of hair to the window hook. Then the King's son came and cried,

"Rapunzel, Rapunzel,
Let down your golden hair."

Then she let the hair down, and the King's son climbed up, but instead of his dearest Rapunzel he found the witch looking at him with glittering eyes.

"Aha!" cried she, mocking him, "you

came for your darling, but the sweet bird sits no longer in the nest, and sings no more; the cat has got her, and will scratch out your eyes as well! Rapunzel is lost to you; you will see her no more."

The King's son was beside himself with grief, and in his agony he sprang from the tower. He escaped with his life, but the thorns on which he fell put out his eyes. Then he wandered blind through the wood, eating nothing but roots and berries, and doing nothing but lament and weep for the loss of his lovely bride.

So he wandered several years in misery until at last he came to the desert place where Rapunzel was living. At first he heard a voice that he thought he knew, and when he reached the place from which it seemed to come Rapunzel knew him, and fell on his neck and wept. And when her tears touched his eyes they became clear again, and he could see with them as well as ever.

Then he took her to his kingdom, where he was received with great joy, and there they lived long and happily.

The Fisherman and his Wife

BY JAKOB AND WILHELM GRIMM

Illustrated by W. T. MARS

THERE was once a fisherman who lived with his wife in a ditch, close by the seaside. The fisherman used to go out all day long a-fishing; and one day, as he sat on the shore with his rod, looking at the shining water and watching his line, all on a sudden his float was dragged away deep under the sea; and in drawing it up he pulled a great fish out of the water. The fish said to him, "Pray let me live. I am an enchanted prince, put me in the water again, and let me go." "Oh!" said the man, "you need not make so many words about the matter; I wish to have nothing to do with a fish that can talk; so swim away as soon as you please." Then he put him back into the water, and the fish darted straight down to the bottom and left a long streak of blood behind him.

When the fisherman went home to his wife in the ditch, he told her how he had caught a great fish, and how it had told him that it was an enchanted prince, and that on hearing it speak he had let it go again. "Did you not ask it for anything?" said the wife. "No," said the man; "what

should I ask for?" "Ah!" said the wife, "we live very wretchedly here in this nasty stinking ditch; do go back, and tell the fish we want a little cottage."

The fisherman did not much like the business: however, he went to the sea, and when he came there the water looked all yellow and green. And he stood at the water's edge, and said:

"O man of the sea!
Come listen to me,
For Alice my wife,
The plague of my life,
Hath sent me to beg a boon of thee!"

Then the fish came swimming to him, and said, "Well, what does she want?"

"Ah!" answered the fisherman, "my wife says that when I had caught you, I ought to have asked you for something before I let you go again; she does not like living any longer in the ditch, and wants a little cottage." "Go home, then," said the fish; "she is in the cottage already." So the man went home; and saw his wife standing at the door of the cottage. "Come in, come in," said she; "is not this much better than the ditch?" And there was a parlor, and a bed-chamber, and a kitchen; and behind the cottage there was a little garden with all sorts of flowers and fruits, and a court-yard full of ducks and chickens. "Ah!" said the fisherman, "how happily we shall live!" "We will try to do so at least," said his wife.

Everything went right for a week or two, and then Dame Alice said, "Husband, there is not room enough in this cottage, the courtyard and garden are a great deal too small; I should like to have a large stone castle to live in; so go to the fish again, and tell him to give us a castle." "Wife," said the fisherman, "I don't like to go to him again, for perhaps he will be angry; we ought to be content with the cottage." "Nonsense!" said the wife; "he will do it willingly; go along and try."

The fisherman went; but his heart was very heavy: and when he came to the sea it looked blue and gloomy, though it was quite calm, and he went close to it, and said:

"O man of the sea!
Come listen to me,
For Alice my wife,
The plague of my life,
Hath sent me to beg a boon of thee!"

"Well, what does she want now?" said the fish. "Ah!" said the man very sorrowfully, "my wife wants to live in a stone castle." "Go home, then," said the fish; "she is standing at the door of it already." So away went the fisherman, and found his wife standing before a great castle. "See," said she, "is not this grand?" With that they went into the castle together, and found a great many servants there, and the rooms all richly furnished and full of golden chairs and tables; and behind the castle was a garden, and a wood half a mile long, full of sheep, and goats, and hares, and deer; and in the courtyard were stables and cowhouses. "Well!" said the man, "now will we live contented and happy in the beautiful castle for the rest of our lives." "Perhaps we may," said the wife; "but let us consider and sleep upon it before we make up our minds." So they went to bed.

Then next morning, when Dame Alice awoke, it was broad daylight, and she jogged the fisherman with her elbow, and said, "Get up, husband, and bestir yourself for we must be king of all the land." "Wife, wife," said the man, "why should we wish to be king? I will not be king." "Then I will," said Alice. "But, wife," answered the fisherman, "how can you be king? The fish cannot make you a king." "Husband," said she, "say no more about it, but go and try; I will be king!" So the man went away, quite sorrowful to think that his wife should want to be king. The sea looked a dark-gray color, and was covered with foam as he cried out:

"O man of the sea!
Come listen to me,
For Alice my wife,
The plague of my life,
Hath sent me to beg a boon of thee!"

"Well, what would she have now?" said the fish. "Alas!" said the man, "my wife wants to be king." "Go home," said the fish; "she is king already."

Then the fisherman went home; and as he came close to the palace, he saw a troop of soldiers, and heard the sound of drums and trumpets; and when he entered in, he saw his wife sitting on a high throne of gold and diamonds, with a golden crown upon her head; and on each side of her stood six beautiful maidens, each a head taller than the other. "Well, wife," said the fisherman, "are you king?" "Yes," said she, "I am king." And when he had looked at her for a long time, he said, "Ah, wife! what a fine thing it is to be king! now we shall never have anything more to wish for." "I don't know how that may be," said she; "never is a long time. I am king, 'tis true, but I begin to be tired of it, and I think I should like to be emperor." "Alas, wife! why should you wish to be emperor?" said the fisherman. "Husband," said she, "go to the fish; I say I will be emperor." "Ah, wife!" replied the fisherman, "the fish cannot make an emperor, and I should not like to ask for such a thing." "I am king," said Alice, "and you are my slave, so go directly!" So the fisherman was obliged to go; and he muttered as he went along, "This will come to no good, it is too much to ask, the fish will be tired at last, and then we shall repent of what we have done." He soon arrived at the sea, and the water was quite black and muddy, and a mighty whirlwind blew over it; but he went to the shore, and said:

> *"O man of the sea!*
> *Come listen to me,*
> *For Alice my wife,*
> *The plague of my life,*
> *Hath sent me to beg a boon of thee!"*

"What would she have now?" said the fish. "Ah!" said the fisherman, "she wants to be emperor." "Go home," said the fish; "she is emperor already."

So he went home again; and as he came near he saw his wife sitting on a very lofty throne made of solid gold, with a great crown on her head full two yards high, and on each side of her stood her guards and attendants in a row, each one smaller than the other, from the tallest giant down to a little dwarf no bigger than a finger. And before her stood princes, and dukes, and earls: and the fisherman went up to her and said, "Wife, are you emperor?" "Yes," said she, "I am emperor."

"Ah!" said the man as he gazed upon her, "what a fine thing it is to be emperor!" "Husband," said she, "why should we stay at being emperor? I will be pope next." "Oh wife, wife!" said he, "how can you be pope? There is but one pope at a time in Christendom." "Husband," said she, "I will be pope this very day." "But," replied the husband, "the fish cannot make you pope." "What nonsense!" said she; "if he can make an emperor, he can make a pope, go and try him." So the fisherman went. But when he came to the shore the wind was raging, and the sea was tossed up and down like boiling water, and the ships were in the greatest distress and danced upon the waves most fearfully; in the middle of the sky there was a little blue, but towards the south it was all red, as if a dreadful storm was rising. At this the fisherman was terribly frightened, and trembled so that his knees knocked together; but he went to the shore and said:

> *"O man of the sea!*
> *Come listen to me,*
> *For Alice my wife,*
> *The plague of my life,*
> *Hath sent me to beg a boon of thee!"*

"What does she want now?" said the fish. "Ah!" said the fisherman, "my wife wants to be pope." "Go home," said the fish, "she is pope already."

Then the fisherman went home, and found his wife sitting on a throne that was two miles high; and she had three great crowns on her head, and around stood all the pomp and power of the Church and on each side were two rows of burning lights, of all sizes, the greatest as large as the highest and biggest tower, and the least no larger than a small rushlight. "Wife," said the fisherman, as he looked

at all this grandeur, "are you pope?" "Yes," said she, "I am pope." "Well, wife," replied he, "it is a grand thing to be pope; and now you must be content, for you can be nothing greater." "I will consider of that," said the wife. Then they went to bed: but Dame Alice could not sleep all night for thinking what she should be next. At last morning came, and the sun rose. "Ah!" thought she as she looked at it through the window, "cannot I prevent the sun rising?" At this she was very angry, and wakened her husband, and said, "Husband, go to the fish and tell him I want to be lord of the sun and moon." The fisherman was half asleep, but the thought frightened him so much, that he started and fell out of bed. "Alas, wife!" said he, "cannot you be content to be pope?" "No," said she, "I am very uneasy, and cannot bear to see the sun and moon rise without my leave. Go to the fish directly."

Then the man went trembling for fear; and as he was going down to the shore a dreadful storm arose, so that the trees and the rocks shook; and the heavens became black, and the lightning played, and the thunder rolled, and you might have seen in the sea great black waves like mountains with a white crown of foam upon them; and the fisherman said:

> "O man of the sea!
> Come listen to me,
> For Alice my wife,
> The plague of my life,
> Hath sent me to beg a boon of thee!"

"What does she want now?" said the fish. "Ah!" said he, "she wants to be lord of the sun and moon." "Go home," said the fish, "to your ditch again!" And there they live to this very day.

The next story was written by the greatest art critic
of the nineteenth century, John Ruskin,
an enormously rich man who gave his
wealth away to help others.
Besides being an art lover and a lover of mankind,
Ruskin was also a moralist.
In "The King of the Golden River" he
not only composed a fairy tale,
but also made it teach a lesson.
The lesson, however, is only implied—
but it should add to your pleasure in following the fortunes
of young and tender-hearted Gluck,
(a name which, translated from German, means Luck),
in meeting the wind disguised as a crusty old man
who exposes Gluck's greedy brothers,
and in the flow of the story itself.
We always like to see good triumph over evil—
and here it emphatically does.

The King of the Golden River

BY JOHN RUSKIN

Illustrated by MAE GERHARD

IN A SECLUDED and mountainous part of Stiria, there was, in old time, a valley of the most surprising and luxuriant fertility. It was surrounded, on all sides, by steep and rocky mountains, rising into peaks, which were always covered with snow, and from which a number of torrents descended in constant cataracts. One of these fell westward, over the face of a crag so high, that, when the sun had set to everything else, and all below was darkness, his beams still shone full upon this waterfall, so that it looked like a shower of gold. It was, therefore, called by the people of the neighborhood the Golden River. It was strange that none of these streams fell into the valley itself. They all descended on the other side of the mountains, and wound away through broad plains and by populous cities. But the clouds were drawn so constantly to the snowy hills, and rested so softly in the circular hollow, that, in time of drought and heat, when all the country was burnt up, there was still rain in the little valley; and its crops were so heavy, and its hay so high, and its apples so red, and its grapes so blue, and its wine so rich, and its honey so sweet, that it was a marvel to everyone who beheld it, and was commonly called the Treasure Valley.

The whole of this little valley belonged to three brothers, called Schwartz, Hans, and Gluck. Schwartz and Hans, the two older brothers, were very ugly men, with overhanging eyebrows and small, dull eyes, which were always half shut, so that you couldn't see into *them,* and always fancied they saw very far into *you.* They lived by farming the Treasure Valley, and very good farmers they were. They killed everything that did not pay for its eating. They shot the blackbirds, because they pecked the fruit; and killed the hedgehogs, lest they should suck the cows; they poisoned the crickets for eating the crumbs in the kitchen; and smothered the cicadas, which used to sing all summer in the lime trees. They worked their servants without any wages, till they would not work any more, and then quarreled with them, and turned them out-of-doors without paying them. It would have been very odd, if, with such a farm, and such a system of farming, they hadn't got very rich; and very rich they *did* get. They generally contrived to keep their corn by them till it was very dear, and then sell it for twice its value; they had heaps of gold lying about on their floors, yet it was never known that they had given so much as a penny or a crust in charity; they never went to Mass; grumbled perpetually at paying tithes; and were, in a word, of so cruel and grinding a temper as to receive from all those with whom they had any dealings the nickname of the "Black Brothers."

The youngest brother, Gluck, was as completely opposed, in both appearance and character, to his seniors as could possibly be imagined or desired. He was not above twelve years old, fair, blue-eyed, and kind in temper to every living thing.

He did not, of course, agree particularly well with his brothers, or rather, they did not agree with *him*. He was usually appointed to the honorable office of turn-spit, when there was anything to roast, which was not often; for, to do the brothers justice, they were hardly less sparing upon themselves than upon other people. At other times he used to clean the shoes, floors, and sometimes the plates, occasionally getting what was left on them, by way of encouragement, and a wholesome quantity of dry blows, by way of education.

Things went on in this manner for a long time. At last came a very wet summer, and everything went wrong in the country round. The hay had hardly been got in, when the haystacks were floated bodily down to the sea by an inundation; the vines were cut to pieces with the hail; the corn was all killed by a black blight; only in the Treasure Valley, as usual, all was safe. As it had rain when there was rain nowhere else, so it had sun when there was sun nowhere else. Everybody came to buy corn at the farm, and went away pouring maledictions on the Black Brothers. They asked what they liked, and got it, except from poor people, who could only beg, and several of whom were starved at their very door, without the slightest regard or notice.

It was drawing towards winter, and very cold weather, when one day the two elder brothers had gone out, with their usual warning to little Gluck, who was left to mind the roast, that he was to let nobody in, and give nothing out. Gluck sat down quite close to the fire, for it was raining very hard, and the kitchen walls were by no means dry or comfortable-looking. He turned and turned, and the roast got nice and brown. "What a pity," thought Gluck, "my brothers never ask anybody to dinner. I'm sure, when they've got such a nice piece of mutton as this, and nobody else has got so much as a piece of dry bread, it would do their hearts good to have somebody to eat it with them."

Just as he spoke, there came a double knock at the house door, yet heavy and dull, as though the knocker had been tied up—more like a puff than a knock.

"It must be the wind," said Gluck; "nobody else would venture to knock double knocks at our door."

No; it wasn't the wind; there it came again very hard, and what was particularly astounding, the knocker seemed to be in a hurry, and not to be in the least afraid of the consequences. Gluck went to the window, opened it, and put his head out to see who it was.

It was the most extraordinary-looking little gentleman that he had ever seen in his life. He had a very large nose, slightly brass-colored; his cheeks were very round, and very red, and might have warranted a supposition that he had been blowing a refractory fire for the last eight-and-forty hours; his eyes twinkled merrily through long silky eyelashes, his moustaches curled twice round like a corkscrew on each side of his mouth, and his hair, of a curious mixed pepper-and-salt color, descended far over his shoulders. He was about four feet six in height, and wore a conical-pointed cap of nearly the same altitude, decorated with a black feather some three feet long. His doublet was prolonged behind into something resembling a violent exaggeration of what is now

termed a "swallow-tail," but was much obscured by the swelling folds of an enormous black, glossy-looking cloak, which must have been very much too long in calm weather, as the wind, whistling round the old house, carried it clear out from the wearer's shoulders to about four times his own length.

Gluck was so perfectly paralyzed by the singular appearance of his visitor, that he remained fixed without uttering a word, until the old gentleman, having performed another, and a more energetic concerto on the knocker, turned round to look after his fly-away cloak. In so doing he caught sight of Gluck's little yellow head jammed in the window, with his mouth and eyes very wide open indeed.

"Hollo!" said the little gentleman, "that's not the way to answer the door; I'm wet; let me in."

To do the little gentleman justice, he *was* wet. His feather hung down between his legs like a beaten puppy's tail, dripping like an umbrella; and from the ends of his moustaches the water was running into his waistcoat pockets, and out again like a mill stream.

"I beg pardon, sir," said Gluck, "I'm very sorry, but I really can't."

"Can't what?" said the old gentleman.

"I can't let you in, sir—I can't indeed; my brothers would beat me to death, sir, if I thought of such a thing. What do you want, sir?"

"Want?" said the old gentleman petulantly, "I want fire and shelter; and there's your great fire there blazing, crackling, and dancing on the wall, with nobody to feel it. Let me in, I say; I only want to warm myself."

Gluck had had his head, by this time, so long out of the window that he began to feel it was really unpleasantly cold; and when he turned, and saw the beautiful fire rustling and roaring, and throwing

112

long bright tongues up the chimney, as if it were licking its chops at the savory smell of the leg of mutton, his heart melted within him that it should be burning away for nothing. "He does look *very* wet," said little Gluck; "I'll just let him in for a quarter of an hour." Round he went to the door and opened it; and as the little gentleman walked in there came a gust of wind through the house that made the old chimneys totter.

"That's a good boy," said the little gentleman. "Never mind your brothers. I'll talk to them."

"Pray, sir, don't do any such thing," said Gluck. "I can't let you stay till they come; they'd be the death of me."

"Dear me," said the old gentleman, "I'm very sorry to hear that. How long may I stay?"

"Only till the mutton's done, sir," replied Gluck, "and it's very brown."

Then the old gentleman walked into

the kitchen and sat himself down on the hob, with the top of his cap accommodated up the chimney, for it was a great deal too high for the roof.

"You'll soon dry there, sir," said Gluck, and sat down again to turn the mutton. But the old gentleman did *not* dry there, but went on drip, drip, dripping among the cinders, and the fire fizzed, and sputtered, and began to look very black and uncomfortable; never was such a cloak; every fold in it ran like a gutter.

"I beg pardon, sir," said Gluck at length, after watching the water spreading in long, quicksilver-like streams over the floor for a quarter of an hour; "mayn't I take your cloak?"

"No, thank you," said the old gentleman.

"Your cap, sir?"

"I am all right, thank you," said the old gentleman rather gruffly.

"But—sir—I'm very sorry," said Gluck, hesitatingly; "but—really, sir—you're putting the fire out."

"It'll take longer to do the mutton then," replied his visitor dryly.

Gluck was very much puzzled by the behavior of his guest; it was such a strange mixture of coolness and humility. He turned away at the string meditatively for another five minutes.

"That mutton looks very nice," said the old gentleman at length. "Can't you give me a little bit?"

"Impossible, sir," said Gluck.

"I'm very hungry," continued the old gentleman; "I've had nothing to eat yesterday, nor today. They surely couldn't miss a bit from the knuckle!"

He spoke in so very melancholy a tone, that it quite melted Gluck's heart. "They

promised me one slice today, sir," said he; "I can give you that, but not a bit more."

"That's a good boy," said the old gentleman again.

Then Gluck warmed a plate, and sharpened a knife. "I don't care if I do get beaten for it," thought he. Just as he had cut a large slice out of the mutton, there came a tremendous rap at the door. The old gentleman jumped off the hob, as if it had suddenly become inconveniently warm. Gluck fitted the slice into the mutton again, with desperate efforts at exactitude, and ran to open the door.

"What did you keep us waiting in the rain for?" said Schwartz, as he walked in, throwing his umbrella in Gluck's face. "Ay! what for, indeed, you little vagabond?" said Hans, administering an educational box on the ear, as he followed his brother into the kitchen.

"Bless my soul!" said Schwartz when he opened the door.

"Amen!" said the little gentleman, who had taken his cap off, and was standing in the middle of the kitchen, bowing with the utmost possible velocity.

"Who's that?" said Schwartz, catching up a rolling pin, and turning to Gluck with a fierce frown.

"I don't know, indeed, brother," said Gluck in great terror.

"How did he get in?" roared Schwartz.

"My dear brother," said Gluck, deprecatingly, "he was so *very* wet!"

The rolling pin was descending on Gluck's head; but, at the instant, the old gentleman interposed his conical cap, on which it crashed with a shock that shook the water out of it all over the room. What was very odd, the rolling pin no sooner

114

touched the cap, than it flew out of Schwartz's hand, spinning like a straw in a high wind, and fell into the corner at the farther end of the room.

"Who are you, sir?" demanded Schwartz, turning upon him.

"What's your business?" snarled Hans.

"I'm a poor old man, sir," the little gentleman began very modestly, "and I saw your fire through the window, and begged shelter for a quarter of an hour."

"Have the goodness to walk out again, then," said Schwartz. "We've quite enough water in our kitchen, without making it a drying house."

"It is a cold day to turn an old man out, sir; look at my gray hairs." They hung down to his shoulders, as I told you before.

"Ay!" said Hans, "there are enough of them to keep you warm. Walk!"

"I'm very, very hungry, sir; couldn't you spare me a bit of bread before I go?"

"Bread, indeed!" said Schwartz; "do you suppose we've nothing to do with our bread but to give it to such red-nosed fellows as you?"

"Why don't you sell your feather?" said Hans, sneeringly. "Out with you!"

"A little bit," said the old gentleman.

"Be off!" said Schwartz.

"Pray, gentlemen."

"Off, and be hanged!" cried Hans, seizing him by the collar. But he had no sooner touched the old gentleman's collar, than away he went after the rolling pin, spinning round and round, till he fell into the corner on top of it. Then Schwartz was very angry, and ran at the old gentleman to turn him out; but he also had hardly touched him, when away he went after Hans and the rolling pin, and hit his head against the wall as he tumbled into

the corner. And so there they lay, all three.

Then the old gentleman spun himself round with velocity in the opposite direction; continued to spin until his long cloak was all wound neatly about him; clapped his cap on his head, very much on one side (for it could not stand upright without going through the ceiling); gave an additional twist to his corkscrew moustaches; and replied with perfect coolness: "Gentlemen, I wish you a very good morning. At twelve o'clock tonight, I'll call again; after such a refusal of hospitality as I have just experienced, you will not be surprised if that visit is the last I ever pay you."

"If ever I catch you here again," muttered Schwartz, coming, half frightened, out of his corner—but, before he could finish his sentence, the old gentleman had shut the house door behind him with a great bang; and there drove past the window, at the same instant, a wreath of ragged cloud, that whirled and rolled away down the valley in all manner of shapes; turning over and over in the air; and melting away at last in a gush of rain.

"A very pretty business, indeed, Mr. Gluck!" said Schwartz. "Dish the mutton, sir. If ever I catch you at such a trick again—bless me, why the mutton's been cut!"

"You promised me one slice, brother, you know," said Gluck.

"Oh! and you were cutting it hot, I suppose, and going to catch all the gravy. It'll be long before I promise you such a thing again. Leave the room, sir; and have the kindness to wait in the coal-cellar till I call you."

Gluck left the room melancholy enough. The brothers ate as much mutton as they could, locked the rest in the cupboard, and proceeded to get very drunk after dinner.

Such a night as it was! Howling wind, and rushing rain, without intermission. The brothers had just sense enough left to put up all the shutters, and double bar the door, before they went to bed. They usually slept in the same room. As the clock struck twelve, they were both awakened by a tremendous crash. Their door burst open with a violence that shook the house from top to bottom.

"What's that?" cried Schwartz, starting up in his bed.

"Only I," said the little gentleman.

The two brothers sat up on their bolster, and stared into the darkness. The room was full of water, and by a misty moonbeam, which found its way through a hole in the shutter, they could see, in the midst of it, an enormous foam globe, spinning round, and bobbing up and down like a cork, on which, as on a most luxurious cushion, reclined the little old gentleman, cap and all. There was plenty of room for it now, for the roof was off.

"Sorry to incommode you," said their visitor, ironically. "I'm afraid your beds are dampish; perhaps you had better go to your brother's room; I've left the ceiling on there."

They required no second admonition, but rushed into Gluck's room, wet through, and in an agony of terror.

"You'll find my card on the kitchen table," the old gentleman called after them. "Remember the *last* visit."

"Pray Heaven it may!" said Schwartz, shuddering. And the foam globe disappeared.

Dawn came at last, and the two broth-ers looked out of Gluck's little window in the morning. The Treasure Valley was one mass of ruin and desolation. The inundation had swept away trees, crops, and cattle, and left, in their stead, a waste of red sand and gray mud. The two brothers crept, shivering and horror-struck, into the kitchen. The water had gutted the whole first floor; corn, money, almost every movable thing had been swept away, and there was left only a small white card on the kitchen table. On it, in large, breezy, long-legged letters were engraved the words:

South-West Wind Esq.

Chapter II

SOUTH-WEST WIND, ESQUIRE, was as good as his word. After the momentous visit above related, he entered the Treasure Valley no more; and, what was worse, he had so much influence with his relations, the West Winds in general, and used it so effectually, that they all adopted a similar line of conduct. So no rain fell in the valley from one year's end to another. Though everything remained green and flourishing in the plains below, the inheritance of the three brothers was a desert. What had once been the richest soil in the kingdom became a shifting heap of red sand; and the brothers, unable longer to contend with the adverse skies, abandoned their valueless patrimony in despair, to seek some means of gaining a livelihood among the cities and people of the plains. All their money was gone, and they had nothing left but some curious, old-fashioned pieces of gold plate, the last remnants of their ill-gotten wealth.

"Suppose we turn goldsmiths?" said Schwartz to Hans, as they entered the large city. "It is a good knave's trade; we can put a great deal of copper into the gold, without anyone's finding it out."

The thought was agreed to be a very good one; they hired a furnace, and turned goldsmiths. But two slight circumstances affected their trade: the first, that people did not approve of the coppered gold; the second, that the two elder brothers, whenever they had sold anything, used to leave little Gluck to mind the furnace, and go and drink out the money in the ale-house next door. So they melted all their gold, without making money enough to buy more, and were at last reduced to one large drinking-mug, which an uncle of his had given to little Gluck, and which he was very fond of, and would not have parted with for the world; though he never drank anything out of it but milk and water. The mug was a very odd mug to look at. The handle was formed of two wreaths of flowing golden hair, so finely spun that it looked more like silk than metal, and these wreaths descended into, and mixed with, a beard and whiskers, of the same exquisite workmanship, which surrounded and decorated a very fierce little face, of the reddest gold imaginable, right in the front of the mug, with a pair of eyes in it which seemed to command its whole circumference. It was impossible to drink out of the mug without being subjected to an intense gaze out of the side of these eyes; and Schwartz positively averred that once, after emptying it full of Rhenish seven-

teen times, he had seen them wink! When it came to the mug's turn to be made into spoons, it half broke poor little Gluck's heart; but the brothers only laughed at him, tossed the mug into the melting-pot, and staggered out to the ale-house; leaving him, as usual, to pour the gold into bars, when it was all ready.

When they were gone, Gluck took a farewell look at his old friend in the melting-pot. The flowing hair was all gone; nothing remained but the red nose, and the sparkling eyes, which looked more malicious than ever. "And no wonder," thought Gluck, "after being treated in that way." He sauntered disconsolately to the window, and sat himself down to catch the fresh evening air, and escape the hot breath of the furnace. Now this window commanded a direct view of the range of mountains, which, as I told you before, overhung the Treasure Valley, and more especially of the peak from which fell the Golden River. It was just at the close of the day, and, when Gluck sat down at the window, he saw the rocks of the mountain tops, all crimson and purple with the sunset; and there were bright tongues of fiery cloud burning and quivering about them; and the river, brighter than all, fell, in a waving column of pure gold, from precipice to precipice, with the double arch of a broad purple rainbow stretched across it, flushing and fading alternately in the wreaths of spray.

"Ah!" said Gluck aloud, after he had looked at it for a little while, "if that river were really all gold, what a nice thing it would be."

"No it wouldn't, Gluck," said a clear metallic voice, close at his ear.

"Bless me! what's that?" exclaimed

Gluck, jumping up. There was nobody there. He looked round the room, and under the table, and a great many times behind him, but there was certainly nobody there, and he sat down again at the window. This time he didn't speak, but he couldn't help thinking again that it would be very convenient if the river were really all gold.

"Not at all, my boy," said the same voice, louder than before.

"Bless me!" said Gluck again, "what *is* that?" He looked again into all the corners and cupboards, and then began turning round and round, as fast as he could, in the middle of the room, thinking there was somebody behind him, when the same voice struck again on his ear. It was singing now very merrily "Lala-lira-la"; no words, only a soft running effervescent melody, something like that of a kettle on the boil. Gluck looked out of the window. No, it was certainly in the house. Upstairs,

and downstairs. No, it was certainly in that very room, coming in quicker time, and clearer notes, every moment: "Lala-lira-la." All at once it struck Gluck that it sounded louder near the furnace. He ran to the opening, and looked in; yes, he saw right, it seemed to be coming, not only out of the furnace, but out of the pot. He uncovered it, and ran back in a great fright, for the pot was certainly singing. He stood in the farthest corner of the room, with his hands up, and his mouth open, for a minute or two, when the singing stopped, and the voice became clear, and pronunciative.

"Hollo!" said the voice.

Gluck made no answer.

"Hollo! Gluck, my boy," said the pot again.

Gluck summoned all his energies, walked straight up to the crucible, drew it out of the furnace, and looked in. The gold was all melted, and its surface as

118

smooth and polished as a river; but instead of reflecting little Gluck's head, as he looked in, he saw meeting his glance, from beneath the gold, the red nose and sharp eyes of his old friend of the mug, a thousand times redder and sharper than ever he had seen them in his life.

"Come, Gluck, my boy," said the voice out of the pot again, "I'm all right; pour me out."

But Gluck was too much astonished to do anything of the kind.

"Pour me out, I say," said the voice, rather gruffly. Still Gluck couldn't move

"*Will* you pour me out?" said the voice, passionately; "I'm too hot."

By a violent effort, Gluck recovered the use of his limbs, took hold of the crucible, and sloped it, so as to pour out the gold. But instead of a liquid stream, there came out, first, a pair of pretty little yellow legs, then some coat tails, then a pair of arms stuck akimbo, and, finally, the well-known head of his friend of the mug; all which articles, uniting as they rolled out, stood up energetically on the floor, in the shape of a little golden dwarf, about a foot and a half high.

"That's right!" said the dwarf, stretching out first his legs, and then his arms, and then shaking his head up and down, and as far round as it would go, for five minutes, without stopping; apparently with the view of ascertaining if he were quite correctly put together, while Gluck stood contemplating him in speechless amazement. He was dressed in a slashed doublet of spun gold, so fine in its texture that the prismatic colors gleamed over it, as if on a surface of mother-of-pearl; and, over this brilliant doublet, his hair and beard fell full half-way to the ground, in

waving curls, so exquisitely delicate that Gluck could hardly tell where they ended; they seemed to melt into air. The features of the face, however, were by no means finished with the same delicacy; they were rather coarse, slightly inclining to coppery in complexion, and indicative, in expression, of a very pertinacious and intractable disposition in their small proprietor. When the dwarf had finished his self-examination, he turned his small sharp eyes full on Gluck, and stared at him deliberately for a minute or two. "No, it wouldn't, Gluck, my boy," said the little man.

This was certainly rather an abrupt and unconnected mode of commencing conversation. It might indeed be supposed to refer to the course of Gluck's thoughts, which had first produced the dwarf's observations out of the pot; but whatever it referred to, Gluck had no inclination to dispute the dictum.

"Wouldn't it, sir?" said Gluck, very mildly and submissively indeed.

"No," said the dwarf, conclusively. "No, it wouldn't." And with that the dwarf pulled his cap hard over his brows, and took two turns of three feet long, up and down the room, lifting his legs up very high, and setting them down very hard. This pause gave time for Gluck to collect his thoughts a little, and, seeing no great reason to view his diminutive visitor with dread, and feeling his curiosity overcome his amazement, he ventured on a question of peculiar delicacy.

"Pray, sir," said Gluck, rather hesitatingly, "were you my mug?"

On which the little man turned sharp round, walked straight up to Gluck, and drew himself up to his full height. "I," said the little man, "am the King of the Golden River." Whereupon he turned about again, and took two more turns, some six feet long, in order to allow time for the consternation which this announcement produced in his auditor to evaporate. After which he again walked up to Gluck, and stood still, as if expecting some comment on his communication.

Gluck determined to say something at all events. "I hope Your Majesty is very well," said Gluck.

"Listen!" said the little man, deigning no reply to this polite inquiry. "I am the King of what you mortals call the Golden River. The shape you saw me in was owing to the malice of a stronger king, from whose enchantments you have this instant freed me. What I have seen of you, and your conduct to your wicked brothers, renders me willing to serve you; therefore attend to what I tell you. Whoever shall climb to the top of that mountain from which you see the Golden River issue, and shall cast into the stream at its source three drops of holy water, for him, and for him only, the river shall turn to gold. But no one failing in his first, can succeed in a second, attempt; and if anyone shall cast unholy water into the river, it will overwhelm him, and he will become a black stone." So saying, the King of the Golden River turned away, and deliberately walked into the center of the hottest flame of the furnace. His figure became red, white, transparent, dazzling —a blaze of intense light—rose, trembled and disappeared. The King of the Golden River had evaporated.

"Oh!" cried poor Gluck, running to look up the chimney after him; "oh, dear, dear, dear me! My mug! my mug! my mug!"

Chapter III

THE KING of the Golden River had hardly made the extraordinary exit related in the last chapter, before Hans and Schwartz came roaring into the house very savagely drunk. The discovery of the total loss of their last piece of plate had the effect of sobering them just enough to enable them to stand over Gluck, beating him very steadily for a quarter of an hour; at the expiration of which period they dropped into a couple of chairs, and requested to know what he had to say for himself. Gluck told them his story, of which of course they did not believe a word. They beat him again, till their arms were tired, and staggered to bed. In the morning, however, the steadiness with which he adhered to his story obtained him some degree of credence; the immediate consequence of which was, that the two brothers, after wrangling a long time on the knotty question, which of them should try his fortune first, drew their swords, and began fighting. The noise of the fray alarmed the neighbors, who, finding they could not pacify the combatants, sent for the constable.

Hans, on hearing this, contrived to escape, and hid himself; but Schwartz was taken before the magistrate, fined for breaking the peace, and, having drunk out his last penny the evening before, was thrown into prison till he should pay.

When Hans heard this, he was much delighted, and determined to set out immediately for the Golden River. How to get the holy water was the question. He went to the priest, but the priest could not give any holy water to so abandoned a character. So Hans went to vespers in the evening for the first time in his life, and, under pretense of crossing himself, stole a cupful, and returned home in triumph.

Next morning he got up before the sun rose, put the holy water into a strong flask, and two bottles of wine and some meat in a basket, slung them over his back, took his alpine staff in his hand, and set off for the mountains.

On his way out of the town he had to pass the prison, and as he looked in at the windows, whom should he see but Schwartz himself peeping out of the bars, and looking very disconsolate.

"Good morning, brother," said Hans; "have you any message for the King of the Golden River?"

Schwartz only gnashed his teeth with rage, and shook the bars with all his strength; but Hans only laughed at him, and advised him to make himself comfortable till he came back again, shouldered his basket, shook the bottle of holy water in Schwartz's face till it frothed again, and marched off in the highest spirits in the world.

It was, indeed, a morning that might have made anyone happy, even with no Golden River to seek for. Level lines of dewy mist lay stretched along the valley, out of which rose the massy mountains— their lower cliffs in pale gray shadow, hardly distinguishable from the floating vapor, but gradually ascending till they caught the sunlight, which ran in sharp touches of ruddy color along the angular crags, and pierced, in long level rays, through their fringes of spear-like pine. Far above shot up red splintered masses of castellated rock, jagged and shivered into myriads of fantastic forms, with here

and there a streak of sunlit snow, traced down their chasms like a line of forked lightning; and, far beyond, and far above all these, fainter than the morning cloud, but purer and changeless, slept, in the blue sky, the utmost peaks of the eternal snow.

The Golden River, which sprang from one of the lower and snowless elevations, was now nearly in shadow; all but the uppermost jets of spray, which rose like slow smoke above the undulating line of the cataract, and floated away in feeble wreaths upon the morning wind.

On this object, and on this alone, Hans' eyes and thought were fixed; forgetting the distance he had to traverse, he set off at an imprudent rate of walking, which greatly exhausted him before he had scaled the first range of the green and low hills. He was, moreover, surprised, on surmounting them, to find that a large glacier, of whose existence, notwithstanding his previous knowledge of the mountains, he had been absolutely ignorant, lay between him and the source of the Golden River. He entered on it with the boldness of a practiced mountaineer; yet he thought he had never traversed so strange or so dangerous a glacier in his life. The ice was excessively slippery, and out of all its chasms came wild sounds of gushing water; not monotonous or low, but changeful and loud, rising occasionally into drifting passages of wild melody, then breaking off into short melancholy tones, or sudden shrieks, resembling those of human voices in distress or pain. The ice was broken into thousands of confused shapes, but none, Hans thought, like the ordinary forms of splintered ice. There seemed a curious *expression* about all their outlines — a perpetual resemblance to living features, distorted and scornful. Myriads of deceitful shadows and lurid lights played and floated about and through the pale blue pinnacles, dazzling and confusing the sight of the traveler; while his ears grew dull and his head giddy with the constant gush and roar of the concealed waters. These painful circumstances increased upon him as he advanced; the ice crashed and yawned into fresh chasms at his feet, tottering spires nodded around him, and fell thundering across his path; and though he had repeatedly faced these dangers on the most terrific glaciers, and in the wildest weather, it was with a new and oppressive feeling of panic terror that he leaped the last chasm, and flung himself, exhausted and shuddering, on the firm turf of the mountain.

He had been compelled to abandon his basket of food, which became a perilous incumbrance on the glacier, and had no means of refreshing himself but by breaking off and eating some of the pieces of ice. This, however, relieved his thirst; an hour's repose recruited his hardy frame, and with the indomitable spirit of avarice he resumed his laborious journey.

His way now lay straight up a ridge of bare red rocks, without a blade of grass to ease the foot, or a projecting angle to afford an inch of shade from the south sun. It was past noon, and the rays beat intensely upon the steep path, while the whole atmosphere was motionless, and penetrated with heat. Intense thirst was soon added to the bodily fatigue with which Hans was now afflicted; glance after glance he cast on the flask of water which hung at his belt. "Three drops are

enough," at last thought he; "I may, at least, cool my lips with it."

He opened the flask, and was raising it to his lips when his eyes fell on an object lying on the rock beside him; he thought it moved. It was a small dog, apparently in the last agony of death from thirst. Its tongue was out, its jaws dry, its limbs extended lifelessly, and a swarm of black ants were crawling about its lips and throat. Its eye moved to the bottle which Hans held in his hand. He raised it, drank, spurned the animal with his foot, and passed on. And he did not know how it was, but he thought that a strange shadow had suddenly come across the blue sky.

The path became steeper and more rugged every moment; and the high hill air, instead of refreshing him, seemed to throw his blood into a fever. The noise of the hill cataracts sounded like mockery in his ears; they were all distant, and his thirst increased every moment. Another hour passed, and he again looked down to the flask at his side; it was half empty, but there was much more than three drops in it. He stopped to open it, and again, as he did so, something moved in the path above him. It was a fair child, stretched nearly lifeless on the rock, its breast heaving with thirst, its eyes closed, and its lips parched and burning. Hans eyed it deliberately, drank, and passed on. And a dark gray cloud came over the sun, and long, snake-like shadows crept up along the mountain sides. Hans struggled on. The sun was sinking, but its descent seemed to bring no coolness; the leaden weight of the dead air pressed upon his brow and heart, but the goal was near. He saw the cataract of the Golden River springing from the hill-side, scarcely five hundred feet above him. He paused for a moment to breathe, and sprang on to complete his task.

At this instant a faint cry fell on his ear. He turned, and saw a gray-haired old man extended on the rocks. His eyes were sunk, his features deadly pale, and gathered into an expression of despair. "Water!" he stretched his arms to Hans and cried, feebly: "Water! I am dying."

"I have none," replied Hans; "thou hast had thy share of life." He strode over the prostrate body, and darted on. And a flash of blue lightning rose out of the east, shaped like a sword; it shook thrice over the whole heaven, and left it dark with one heavy, impenetrable shade. The sun was setting; it plunged towards the horizon like a red-hot ball.

The roar of the Golden River rose on Hans' ear. He stood at the brink of the chasm through which it ran. Its waves were filled with the red glory of the sunset; they shook their crests like tongues of fire, and flashes of bloody light gleamed along their foam. Their sound came mightier and mightier on his senses; his brain grew giddy with the prolonged thunder. Shuddering, he drew the flask from his girdle and hurled it into the center of the torrent. As he did so, an icy chill shot through his limbs; he staggered, shrieked, and fell. The waters closed over his cry. And the moaning of the river rose wildly into the night, as it gushed over THE BLACK STONE.

Chapter IV

POOR LITTLE GLUCK waited very anxiously alone in the house for Hans' return. Finding he did not come back, he was terribly frightened, and went and told Schwartz in the prison all that had happened. Then Schwartz was very much pleased, and said that Hans must certainly have been turned into a black stone, and he should have all the gold to himself. But Gluck was very sorry, and cried all night. When he got up in the morning, there was no bread in the house, nor any money; so Gluck went and hired himself to another goldsmith, and he worked so hard, and so neatly, and so long every day, that he soon got money enough together to pay his brother's fine, and he went, and gave it all to Schwartz, and Schwartz got out of prison. Then Schwartz was quite pleased, and said he should have some of the gold of the river. But Gluck only begged he would go and see what had become of Hans.

Now when Schwartz had heard that Hans had stolen the holy water, he thought to himself that such a proceeding might not be considered altogether correct by the King of the Golden River, and determined to manage matters better. So he took some more of Gluck's money, and went to a bad priest, who gave him some holy water very readily for it. Then Schwartz was sure it was all quite right. So Schwartz got up early in the morning before the sun rose, and took some bread and wine, in a basket, and put his holy water in a flask, and set off for the mountains. Like his brother, he was much surprised at the sight of the glacier, and had great difficulty in crossing it, even after leaving his basket behind him. The day was cloudless, but not bright; there was a heavy purple haze hanging over the sky, and the hills looked lowering and gloomy. And as Schwartz climbed the steep rock path, the thirst came upon him, as it had upon his brother, until he lifted his flask to his lips to drink. Then he saw the fair child lying near him on the rocks, and it cried to him, and moaned for water.

"Water, indeed," said Schwartz; "I haven't half enough for myself," and passed on. And as he went he thought the sunbeams grew more dim, and he saw a low bank of black cloud rising out of the west; and, when he had climbed for another hour, the thirst overcame him again, and he would have drunk. Then he saw the old man lying before him on the path, and heard him cry out for water. "Water, indeed," said Schwartz, "I haven't half enough for myself," and on he went.

Then again the light seemed to fade from before his eyes, and he looked up, and, behold, a mist, of the color of blood, had come over the sun; and the bank of black cloud had risen very high, and its edges were tossing and tumbling like the waves of an angry sea. And they cast long shadows, which flickered over Schwartz's path.

Then Schwartz climbed for another hour, and again his thirst returned; and as he lifted his flask to his lips, he thought he saw his brother Hans lying exhausted on the path before him, and, as he gazed, the figure stretched its arms to him, and cried for water. "Ha, ha," laughed Schwartz, "are you there? Remember the prison bars, my boy. Water, indeed! do you suppose I carried it all the way up here for *you?*" And he strode over the figure; yet, as he passed, he thought he saw a strange expression of mockery about its lips. And, when he had gone a few yards farther, he looked back; but the figure was not there.

And a sudden horror came over Schwartz, he knew not why; but the thirst for gold prevailed over his fear, and he rushed on. And the bank of black cloud rose to the zenith, and out of it came bursts of spiry lightning, and waves of darkness seemed to heave and float between their flashes over the whole heavens. And the sky where the sun was setting was all level, and like a lake of blood; and a strong wind came out of that sky, tearing its crimson clouds into fragments, and scattering them far into the darkness. And when Schwartz stood by the brink of the Golden River, its waves were black, like thunder-clouds, but their foam was like fire; and the roar of the waters below and the thunder above met, as he cast the flask into the stream. And, as he did so, the lightning glared in his eyes, and the earth gave way beneath him, and the waters closed over his cry. And the moaning of the river rose wildly into the night, as it gushed over the

TWO BLACK STONES.

Chapter V

WHEN GLUCK found that Schwartz did not come back, he was very sorry, and did not know what to do. He had no money, and was obliged to go and hire himself again to the goldsmith, who worked him very hard, and gave him very little money. So, after a month or two, Gluck grew tired and made up his mind to go and try his fortune with the Golden River. "The little king looked very kind," thought he. "I don't think he will turn me into a black stone." So he went to the priest, and the priest gave him some holy water as soon as he asked for it. Then

Gluck took some bread in his basket, and the bottle of water, and set off very early for the mountains.

If the glacier had occasioned a great deal of fatigue to his brothers, it was twenty times worse for him, who was neither so strong nor so practiced on the mountains. He had several very bad falls, lost his basket and bread, and was very much frightened at the strange noises under the ice. He lay a long time to rest on the grass, after he had got over, and began to climb the hill just in the hottest part of the day. When he had climbed for an hour he got dreadfully thirsty, and was going to drink, like his brothers, when he saw an old man coming down the path above him, looking very feeble, and leaning on a staff. "My son," said the old man, "I am faint with thirst, give me some of that water." Then Gluck looked at him, and when he saw that he was pale and weary, he gave him the water. "Only pray don't drink it all," said Gluck. But the old man drank a great deal, and gave him back the bottle two-thirds empty. Then he bade him good speed, and Gluck went on again merrily. And the path became easier to his feet, and two or three blades of grass appeared upon it, and some grasshoppers began singing on the bank beside it; and Gluck thought he had never heard such merry singing.

Then he went on for another hour, and the thirst increased on him so that he thought he should be forced to drink. But, as he raised the flask, he saw a little child lying panting by the road-side, and it cried out piteously for water. Then Gluck struggled with himself, and determined to bear the thirst a little longer; and he put the bottle to the child's lips, and it drank all but a few drops. Then it smiled on him, and got up, and ran down the hill; and Gluck looked after it, till it became as small as a little star, and then turned, and began climbing again. And then there were all kinds of sweet flowers growing on the rocks, bright green moss, with pale-pink starry flowers, and soft belled gentians, more blue than the sky at its deepest, and pure white transparent lilies. And crimson and purple butterflies darted hither and thither, and the sky sent down such pure light that Gluck had never felt so happy in his life.

Yet, when he had climbed for another hour, his thirst became intolerable again; and when he looked at his bottle he saw that there were only five or six drops left in it, and he could not venture to drink. As he was hanging the flask to his belt again, he saw a little dog lying on the rocks, gasping for breath — just as Hans had seen it on the day of his ascent. And Gluck stopped and looked at it, and then at the Golden River, not five hundred yards above him; and he thought of the dwarf's words, "that no one could succeed, except in his first attempt"; and he tried to pass the dog, but it whined piteously, and Gluck stopped again. "Poor beastie," said Gluck, "it'll be dead when I come down again if I don't help it." Then he looked closer and closer at it, and its eye turned on him so mournfully that he could not stand it. "Confound the King and his gold too," said Gluck; and he opened the flask and poured all the water into the dog's mouth.

The dog sprang up and stood on its hind legs. Its tail disappeared, its ears became long, longer, silky, golden; its nose became very red; its eyes became

very twinkling; in three seconds the dog was gone, and before Gluck stood his old acquaintance, the King of the Golden River.

"Thank you," said the monarch; "but don't be frightened, it's all right;" for Gluck showed manifest symptoms of consternation at this unlooked-for reply to his last observation. "Why didn't you come before," continued the dwarf, "instead of sending me those rascally brothers of yours, for me to have the trouble of turning into stones? Very hard stones they make too."

"Oh, dear me!" said Gluck, "have you really been so cruel?"

"Cruel!" said the dwarf. "They poured unholy water into my stream; do you suppose I'm going to allow that?"

"Why," said Gluck, "I am sure, sir— Your Majesty, I mean—they got the water out of the church font."

"Very probably," replied the dwarf; "but," and his countenance grew stern as he spoke, "the water which has been re-fused to the cry of the weary and dying is unholy, though it had been blessed by every saint in heaven; and the water which is found in the vessel of mercy is holy, though it had been defiled with corpses."

So saying, the dwarf stooped and plucked a lily that grew at his feet. On its white leaves there hung three drops of clear dew. And the dwarf shook them into the flask which Gluck held in his hand. "Cast these into the river," he said, "and descend on the other side of the mountains into the Treasure Valley. And so good speed."

As he spoke, the figure of the dwarf became indistinct. The playing colors of his robe formed themselves into a prismatic mist of dewy light; he stood for an instant veiled with them as with the belt of a broad rainbow. The colors grew faint, the mist rose into the air; the monarch had evaporated.

And Gluck climbed to the brink of the Golden River, and its waves were as clear

as crystal, and as brilliant as the sun. And when he cast the three drops of dew into the stream, there opened where they fell a small circular whirlpool, into which the waters descended with a musical noise.

Gluck stood watching it for some time, very much disappointed, because not only the river was not turned into gold, but its waters seemed much diminished in quantity. Yet he obeyed his friend the dwarf, and descended the other side of the mountains, toward the Treasure Valley; and, as he went, he thought he heard the noise of water working its way under the ground. And, when he came in sight of the Treasure Valley, behold, a river like the Golden River was springing from a new cleft of the rocks above it, and was flowing in innumerable streams among the dry heaps of red sand.

And as Gluck gazed, fresh grass sprang beside the new streams, and creeping plants grew and climbed among the moistening soil. Young flowers opened suddenly along the river sides, as stars leap

out when twilight is deepening, and thickets of myrtle and tendrils of vine cast lengthening shadows over the valley as they grew. And thus the Treasure Valley became a garden again, and the inheritance, which had been lost by cruelty, was regained by love.

And Gluck went and dwelt in the valley, and the poor were never driven from his door; so that his barns became full of corn, and his house of treasure. And, for him, the river had, according to the dwarf's promise, become a River of Gold.

And, to this day, the inhabitants of the valley point out the place where the three drops of holy dew were cast into the stream, and trace the course of the Golden River under the ground until it emerges in the Treasure Valley. And at the top of the cataract of the Golden River are still to be seen TWO BLACK STONES, round which the waters howl mournfully every day at sunset; and these stones are still called by the people of the valley THE BLACK BROTHERS.

127

In his famous novels, Charles Dickens created characters
humorous and humane, like
Oliver Twist and David Copperfield,
who are as familiar to us as any characters in literature.
Dickens was devoted to simple people
and was a champion of the poor and oppressed.
Even in so light a fairy tale as "The Magic Fishbone,"
he pictured a family with many children and
too little means to support them.
The ironical story is a curious combination of
real life drudgery and fairy tale elements
that might well be in the daydreams of a girl like Alicia.
In her imagination Alicia is a true Princess,
her humble family is a royal one—
and, of course, she has a fairy godmother.

The Magic Fishbone

BY CHARLES DICKENS
Illustrated by W. T. MARS

THERE was once a king, and he had a queen. They had nineteen children and were always having more. Seventeen of the children took care of the baby; and Alicia, the eldest, took care of them all. Their ages varied from seven years to seven months.

One day the king was going to the office, when he stopped at Mr. Pickle's, the fishmonger's, to buy a pound and a half of salmon not too near the tail.

The king then went on towards the office in a melancholy mood, for payday was such a long way off, and his children were growing out of their clothes.

Just then a rich-looking old lady came trotting up.

"King Watkins the First, I believe?" said the old lady.

"Watkins," replied the king, "is my name."

"Listen. You are going to the office," said the old lady.

It instantly flashed upon the king that she must be a fairy, or how could she know that?

129

"You are right," said the old lady, answering his thoughts. "I am the good Fairy Grandmarina. Listen! When you return home to dinner, politely invite the Princess Alicia to have some of the salmon you bought just now. Then she will leave a fishbone on her plate. Tell her to dry it, and to rub it, and to polish it, till it shines like mother-of-pearl, and to take care of it as a present from me.

"Tell the Princess Alicia," said the fairy, "that the fishbone is a magic present which can only be used once; but that it will bring her, just once, whatever she wishes for, provided she wishes for it at the right time."

With those words, Grandmarina vanished, and the king went on and on, till he came to the office. There he wrote and wrote and wrote, till it was time to go home.

Then he invited the Princess Alicia, as the fairy had directed him, to eat some salmon. And when she had enjoyed it very much, he saw the fishbone on her plate, and he delivered the fairy's message, and the Princess Alicia took care to dry the bone, and to rub it, and to polish it, till it shone like mother-of-pearl.

And so, when the queen was going to get up in the morning, she said, "Oh, dear me, dear me, my head, my head!" and then she fainted away.

The Princess Alicia was very much alarmed when she saw her royal mamma in this state, and she rang the bell for Peggy, which was the name of the lord chamberlain. But remembering where the smelling-bottle was, she climbed on a chair and got it; and after that she climbed on another chair by the bedside, and held the smelling-bottle to the queen's nose; and after that she got some water and wet the queen's forehead; and, in short, when the lord chamberlain came in, that dear old woman said to the little princess, "I couldn't have done it better myself!"

But that was not the worst of the good queen's illness. Oh, no! She was very ill indeed, for a long time. The Princess Alicia kept the seventeen young princes and princesses quiet, and dressed and undressed the baby, and made the kettle boil, and heated the soup, and swept the hearth, and poured out the medicine, and nursed the queen. For there were not many servants at that palace for three reasons: because the king was short of money, because a raise in his salary never seemed to come, and because payday was far off.

But on the morning when the queen fainted away, where was the magic fishbone? Why, there it was in the Princess Alicia's pocket! She had almost taken it out to bring the queen to life again, when she put it back, and looked for the smelling-bottle.

After the queen had come out of her swoon, the Princess Alicia hurried upstairs to tell a secret to her friend the duchess. People thought she was a doll, but Alicia knew she was really a duchess.

"Alicia," said the king, one evening, when she wished him good night.

"Yes, Papa."

"What is become of the magic fishbone?"

"In my pocket, Papa."

"I thought you had lost it?"

"Oh, no, Papa!"

"Or forgotten it?"

"No, indeed, Papa."

And so another time the little snapping dog, next door, made a rush at one of the young princes, and he put his hand through a pane of glass, and bled, bled, bled. Then the sixteen other young princes and princesses saw him and screamed themselves black in their sixteen faces all at once.

But the Princess Alicia put her hands over all their sixteen mouths, one after another, and persuaded them to be quiet because of the sick queen. And then she put the wounded prince's hand in a basin of cold water.

Then she said to two chubby-legged princes, "Bring me in the royal rag-bag: I must snip and stitch and cut and contrive." So these two young princes tugged at the royal rag-bag, and she made a bandage, and it fitted beautifully; and so when it was all done, she saw the king, her papa, looking on by the door.

"Alicia."

"Yes, Papa."

"Where is the magic fishbone?"

"In my pocket, Papa."

"I thought you had lost it?"

"Oh, no, Papa!"

"Or forgotten it?"

"No, indeed, Papa."

After that, she ran upstairs to the duchess, and told her what had happened, and told her the secret over again; and the duchess shook her flaxen curls and laughed with her rosy lips.

Well! and so another time the baby fell under the grate, and it gave him a swelled face and a black eye.

The way the poor little darling came to tumble was that he was out of the Princess Alicia's lap just as she was beginning to peel the turnips for the broth for dinner; and the way she came to be doing that was, that the king's cook had run away that morning with her own true love, who was a very tall but very tipsy soldier.

Then the seventeen young princes and princesses, who cried at everything that happened, cried and roared. But the Princess Alicia (who couldn't help crying a little herself) said, "Hold your tongues, you wicked little monkeys, every one of you, while I examine the baby."

Then she examined the baby, and found that he hadn't broken anything, and she held a cold cloth to his poor dear eye, and he presently fell asleep in her arms.

Then she said to the seventeen princes and princesses, "I am afraid to let him down yet, lest he should wake and feel pain; be good and you shall all be cooks."

They jumped for joy when they heard that, and began making themselves cooks' caps out of old newspapers. So to one she gave the salt-box, and to one she gave the barley, and to one she gave the herbs, and to one she gave the turnips, and to one she gave the carrots, and to one she gave the onions, and to one she gave the spice-box, till they were all cooks, and all running about at work, she sitting in the middle smothered in the great coarse apron, nursing baby.

By and by the broth was done; and the baby woke up, smiling like an angel, and was trusted to the sedatest princess to hold.

When the broth came tumbling out, steaming beautifully, and smelling like a nosegay good to eat, they clapped their hands. That made the baby clap his hands; and that, and his looking as if he

had a comic toothache, made all the princes and princesses laugh.

So the Princess Alicia said, "Laugh and be good; and after dinner we will make him a nest on the floor in a corner, and he shall sit in his nest and see a dance of eighteen cooks." That delighted the young princes and princesses, and they ate up all the broth, and washed up all the plates and dishes, and cleared away, and pushed the table into a corner; and then they in their cooks' caps and the Princess Alicia in her apron danced a dance of eighteen cooks before the angelic baby.

And so then, once more the Princess Alicia saw King Watkins the First, her father, standing in the doorway looking on, and he said, "Where is the magic fishbone, Alicia?"

"In my pocket, Papa."

"I thought you had lost it?"

"Oh, no, Papa!"

"Or forgotten it?"

"No, indeed, Papa."

The king then sighed so heavily, and seemed so low-spirited, that the seventeen princes and princesses crept softly out of the kitchen, and left him alone with the Princess Alicia and the angelic baby.

"What is the matter, Papa?"

"I am dreadfully poor, my child."

"Have you no money at all, Papa?"

"None, my child."

"Is there no way of getting any, Papa?"

"No way," said the king.

"Papa," said she, "when we have tried very hard, and tried all ways, we must have done our very, very best. And when we have done our very, very best, Papa, and that is not enough, then I think the

right time must have come for asking help of others."

This was the very secret connected with the magic fishbone, which she had found out for herself from the good Fairy Grandmarina's words, and which she had so often whispered to her beautiful and fashionable doll, the duchess.

So she took out of her pocket the magic fishbone that had been dried and rubbed and polished till it shone like mother-of-pearl; and she gave it one little kiss and wished it was payday. And immediately it was payday; and the king's salary came rattling down the chimney, and bounced into the middle of the floor.

Immediately afterwards the good Fairy Grandmarina came riding in, in a carriage and four (peacocks), with Mr. Pickle's boy up behind, dressed in silver and gold, with a cocked hat, powdered hair, pink silk stockings, a jewelled cane, and a nosegay.

The Princess Alicia embraced her; and then Grandmarina turned to the king, and said rather sharply, "Are you good?"

The king said he hoped so.

"I suppose you know the reason now why my goddaughter here," kissing the princess again, "did not apply to the fishbone sooner?" said the fairy.

The king made a shy bow.

"Ah! but you didn't then?" said the fairy.

The king made a shyer bow.

"Any more questions to ask?" said the fairy.

The king said no, and he was very sorry.

"Be good, then," said the fairy, "and live happy ever afterwards."

Then Grandmarina waved her fan, and the queen came in most splendidly

133

dressed; and the seventeen young princes and princesses came in, newly fitted out from top to toe, with tucks in everything to admit of its being let out.

After that, the fairy tapped the Princess Alicia with her fan. The smothering coarse apron flew away, and she appeared exquisitely dressed, like a little bride, with a wreath of orange blossoms and a silver veil.

After that, the kitchen dresser changed of itself into a wardrobe, made of beautiful woods and gold and looking glass, which was full of dresses of all sorts, all for her and all exactly fitting her. After that, the angelic baby came in running alone, with his face and eye not a bit worse, but much the better.

A little whispering took place between the fairy and the duchess; and then the fairy said out loud, "Yes, I thought she would have told you." Grandmarina then turned to the king and queen, and said, "We are going in search of Prince Certainpersonio. The pleasure of your company is requested at church in half an hour precisely."

So she and the Princess Alicia got into the carriage; and Mr. Pickle's boy handed in the duchess, who sat by herself on the opposite seat; and then Mr. Pickle's boy put up the steps and got up behind, and peacocks flew away with their tails behind.

Prince Certainpersonio was sitting by himself, eating barley-sugar, and waiting to be ninety. When he saw the peacocks, followed by the carriage, coming in at the window he knew something unusual was going to happen.

"Prince," said Grandmarina, "I bring you your bride."

The moment the fairy said those words, Prince Certainpersonio's face left off being sticky, and his jacket and corduroys changed into peach-bloom velvet, and his hair curled, and a cap and feather flew in like a bird and settled on his head. He got into the carriage by the fairy's invitation and smiled at the duchess, whom he had seen before.

The marriage in the church was ever so beautiful! The duchess was bridesmaid and looked on at the ceremony from the pulpit, where she was propped up by the cushion of the desk.

Grandmarina gave a magnificent wedding-feast afterwards. The wedding-cake was delicately ornamented with white satin ribbons, frosted silver, and white lilies, and was forty-two yards round.

When Grandmarina had drunk a toast to the young people, and Prince Certainpersonio had made a speech, and everybody had cried, "Hip, hip, hip, hurrah!" Grandmarina announced to the king and the queen that in the future there would be eight paydays every year, except in leap year, when there would be ten.

She then turned to Certainpersonio and Alicia, and said, "My dears, you will have thirty-five children, and they will all be good and beautiful. Seventeen of your children will be boys, and eighteen will be girls. They will never have the measles and will have recovered from the whooping cough before being born."

"It only remains," said Grandmarina in conclusion, "to make an end of the fishbone."

So she took it from the hand of the Princess Alicia, and it instantly vanished, before it could possibly be snapped up by the little pugdog next door.

Most people believe that "Aladdin and the Wonderful Lamp"
belongs to The Arabian Nights' Entertainments.
Actually, it is not to be found in the original assembly.
When a French translator of the tales made a selection,
he filled out his volume with a few stories
in the same Oriental vein.
One of these was the tale of Aladdin.
No one knows where the Frenchman got the plot of the story;
scholars have been unable to learn whether he found it
in some obscure manuscript,
or heard it somewhere, or made it up himself.

Aladdin and the Wonderful Lamp
From The Arabian Nights' Entertainments
EDITED BY ANDREW LANG
Illustrated by LOWELL HESS

THERE once lived a poor tailor who had a son called Aladdin, a careless, idle boy who would do nothing but play ball all day long in the streets with little idle boys like himself. This so grieved the father that he died; yet, in spite of his mother's tears and prayers, Aladdin did not mend his ways.

One day, when he was playing in the streets as usual, a stranger asked him his age, and if he was not the son of Mustapha the tailor. "I am, sir," replied Aladdin; "but he died a long while ago." On this the stranger, who was a famous African magician, fell on his neck and kissed him, saying, "I am your uncle, and knew you from your likeness to my brother. Go to your mother and tell her I am coming." Aladdin ran home and told his mother of his newly found uncle. "Indeed, child," she said, "your father had a brother, but I always thought he was dead." However, she prepared supper, and bade Aladdin seek his uncle, who came laden with wine

and fruit. He presently fell down and kissed the place where Mustapha used to sit, bidding Aladdin's mother not to be surprised at not having seen him before, as he had been forty years out of the country. He then turned to Aladdin, and asked him his trade, at which the boy hung his head, while his mother burst into tears. On learning that Aladdin was idle and would learn no trade, he offered to take a shop for him and stock it with merchandise. Next day he bought Aladdin a fine suit of clothes and took him all over the city, showing him the sights, and brought him home at nightfall to his mother, who was overjoyed to see her son so fine.

The next day the magician led Aladdin into some beautiful gardens a long way outside the city gates. They sat down by a fountain and the magician pulled a cake from his girdle, which he divided between them. They then journeyed onward till they almost reached the mountains. Aladdin was so tired that he begged to go back, but the magician beguiled him with pleasant stories, and led him on in spite of himself. At last they came to two mountains divided by a narrow valley. "We will go no farther," said the false uncle. "I will show you something wonderful; only do you gather up sticks while I kindle a fire." When it was lit the magician threw on it a powder he had about him, at the same time saying some magical words. The earth trembled a little and opened in front of them, disclosing a square flat stone with a brass ring in the middle to raise it by. Aladdin tried to run away, but the magician caught him and gave him a blow that knocked him down. "What have I done, Uncle?" he said piteously; whereupon the magician said more kindly: "Fear nothing, but obey me. Beneath this stone lies a treasure which is to be yours, and no one else may touch it, so you must do exactly as I tell you." At the word treasure Aladdin forgot his fears, and grasped the ring as he was told, saying the names of his father and grandfather. The stone came up quite easily, and some steps appeared. "Go down," said the magician; "at the foot of those steps you will find an

open door leading into three large halls. Tuck up your gown and go through them without touching anything, or you will die instantly. These halls lead into a garden of fine fruit trees. Walk on until you come to a niche in a terrace where stands a lighted lamp. Pour out the oil it contains, and bring it to me." He drew a ring from his finger and gave it to Aladdin, bidding him prosper.

Aladdin found everything as the magician had said, gathered some fruit off the trees, and having got the lamp, arrived at the mouth of the cave. The magician cried out in a great hurry: "Make haste and give me the lamp." This Aladdin refused to do until he was out of the cave. The magician flew into a terrible passion and, throwing some more powder on to the fire, he said something, and the stone rolled back into its place.

The magician left China forever, which plainly showed that he was no uncle of Aladdin's, but a cunning magician, who had read in his magic books of a wonderful lamp which would make him the most powerful man in the world. Though he alone knew where to find it, he could only receive it from the hand of another. He had picked out the foolish Aladdin for this purpose, intending to get the lamp and kill him afterward.

For two days Aladdin remained in the dark, crying and lamenting. At last he clasped his hands in prayer, and in so doing rubbed the ring, which the magician had forgotten to take from him. Immediately an enormous and frightful genie rose out of the earth, saying: "What wouldst thou with me? I am the Slave of the Ring, and will obey thee in all things." Aladdin fearlessly replied: "Deliver me from this place!" whereupon the earth opened, and he found himself outside. As soon as his eyes could bear the light he went home, but fainted on the threshold. When he came to himself he told his mother what had passed, and showed her the lamp and the fruits he had gathered in the garden, which were, in reality, precious stones. He then asked for some food. "Alas, child!" she said. "I have nothing in the house, but I have spun a little cotton and will go and sell it." Aladdin bade her keep her cotton, for he would sell the lamp instead. As it was very dirty she began to rub it, that it might fetch a higher price. Instantly a hideous genie appeared, and asked what she would have. She fainted away, but Aladdin, snatching the lamp, said boldly: "Fetch me something to eat!" The genie returned with a silver bowl, twelve silver plates containing rich meats, two silver cups, and two bottles of wine. Aladdin's mother, when she came to herself, said: "Whence comes this splendid feast?" "Ask not, but eat," replied Aladdin. So they sat at breakfast till it was dinnertime, and Aladdin told his mother about the lamp. She begged him to sell it, and have nothing to do with devils. "No," said Aladdin, "since chance hath made us aware of its virtues, we will use it, and the ring likewise, which I shall always wear on my finger." When they had eaten all the genie had brought, Aladdin sold one of the silver plates, and so on until none were left. He then had recourse to the genie, who gave him another set of plates, and thus they lived for many years.

One day Aladdin heard an order from the Sultan proclaiming that everyone was to stay at home and close his shutters while the Princess, his daughter, went to and from the bath. Aladdin was seized by a desire to see her face, which was very difficult as she always went veiled. He hid himself behind the door of the bath, and peeped through a chink. The Princess lifted her veil as she went in, and looked so beautiful that Aladdin fell in love with her at first sight. He went home so changed that his mother was frightened. He told her he loved the Princess so deeply that he could not live without her, and meant to ask her hand in marriage of her father. His mother, on hearing this, burst out laughing, but Aladdin at last prevailed upon her to go before the Sultan and carry his request. She fetched a napkin and laid in it the magic fruits from the enchanted garden, which sparkled and shone like the most beautiful jewels. She took these with her to please the Sultan, and set out, trusting in the lamp. The Grand Vizier and the lords of council had just gone in as she entered the hall and placed herself in front of the Sultan. He, however, took no notice of her. She went every day for a week, and stood in the same place. When the council broke up on the sixth day the Sultan said to his Vizier: "I see a certain woman in the audience chamber every day carrying something in a napkin. Call her next time, that I may find out what she wants." Next day, at a sign from the Vizier, she went up to the foot of the throne and remained kneeling till the Sultan said to her: "Rise, good woman, and tell me what you want." She hesitated, so the Sultan sent away all but the Vizier, and bade her speak frankly, promising to forgive her beforehand for anything she might say. She then told him of her son's violent love for the Prin-

cess. "I prayed him to forget her," she said, "but in vain; he threatened to do some desperate deed if I refused to go and ask Your Majesty for the hand of the Princess. Now I pray you to forgive not me alone, but my son Aladdin." The Sultan asked her kindly what she had in the napkin, whereupon she unfolded the jewels and presented them. He was thunderstruck, and turning to the Vizier said: "What sayest thou? Ought I not to bestow the Princess on one who values her at such a price?" The Vizier, who wanted her for his own son, begged the Sultan to withhold her for three months, in the course of which he hoped his son would contrive to make him a richer present. The Sultan granted this, and told Aladdin's mother that, though he consented to the marriage, she must not appear before him again for three months.

Aladdin waited patiently for nearly three months, but after two had elapsed, his mother, going into the city to buy oil, found everyone rejoicing, and asked what was going on. "Do you not know," was the answer, "that the son of the Grand Vizier is to marry the Sultan's daughter tonight?" Breathless, she ran and told Aladdin, who was overwhelmed at first, but presently bethought him of the lamp. He rubbed it, and the genie appeared, saying, "What is thy will?" Aladdin replied: "The Sultan, as thou knowest, has broken his promise to me, and the Vizier's son is to have the Princess. My command is that tonight you bring hither the bride and bridegroom." "Master, I obey," said the genie. Aladdin then went to his chamber, where, sure enough, at midnight the genie transported the bed containing the Vizier's son and the Princess. "Take this

new-married man," he said, "and put him outside in the cold, and return at daybreak." Whereupon the genie took the Vizier's son out of bed, leaving Aladdin with the Princess. "Fear nothing," Aladdin said to her; "you are my wife, promised to me by your unjust father, and no harm shall come to you." The Princess was too frightened to speak, and passed the most miserable night of her life, while

Aladdin lay down beside her and slept soundly. At the appointed hour the genie fetched in the shivering bridegroom, laid him in his place, and transported the bed back to the palace.

Presently the Sultan came to wish his daughter good morning. The unhappy Vizier's son jumped up and hid himself, while the Princess would not say a word, and was very sorrowful. The Sultan sent her mother to her, who said: "How comes it, child, that you will not speak to your father? What has happened?" The Princess sighed deeply, and at last told her mother how, during the night, the bed had been carried into some strange house, and what had passed there. Her mother did not believe her in the least, but bade her rise and consider it an idle dream.

The following night exactly the same thing happened, and next morning, on the Princess's refusal to speak, the Sultan threatened to cut off her head. She then confessed all, bidding him to ask the Vizier's son if it were not so. The Sultan told the Vizier to ask his son, who owned the truth, adding that, dearly as he loved the Princess, he had rather die than go

141

through another such fearful night, and wished to be separated from her. His wish was granted, and there was an end to feasting and rejoicing.

When the three months were over, Aladdin sent his mother to remind the Sultan of his promise. She stood in the same place as before, and the Sultan, who had forgotten Aladdin, at once remembered him, and sent for her. On seeing her poverty the Sultan felt less inclined than ever to keep his word, and asked his Vizier's advice, who counseled him to set so high a value on the Princess that no man living could come up to it. The Sultan then turned to Aladdin's mother, saying: "Good woman, a sultan must remember his promises, and I will remember mine, but your son must first send me forty basins of gold brimful of jewels, carried by forty black slaves, led by as many white ones, splendidly dressed. Tell him that I await his answer." The mother of Aladdin bowed low and went home, thinking all was lost. She gave Aladdin the message, adding: "He may wait long enough for your answer!" "Not so long, Mother, as you think," her son replied. "I would do a great deal more than that for the Princess." He summoned the genie, and in a few moments the eighty slaves arrived, and filled up the small house and garden. Aladdin made them set out to the palace, two and two, followed by his mother. They were so richly dressed, with such splendid jewels in their girdles, that everyone crowded to see them and the basins of gold they carried on their heads. They entered the palace, and after kneeling before the Sultan, stood in a half circle round the throne with their arms crossed, while Aladdin's mother presented them

to the Sultan. He hesitated no longer, but said: "Good woman, return and tell your son that I wait for him with open arms." She lost no time in telling Aladdin, bidding him make haste. But Aladdin first called the genie. "I want a scented bath," he said, "a richly embroidered habit, a horse surpassing the Sultan's, and twenty slaves to attend me. Besides this, six slaves, beautifully dressed, to wait on my mother; and lastly, ten thousand pieces of gold in ten purses." No sooner said than done. Aladdin mounted his horse and passed through the streets, the slaves strewing gold as they went. Those who had played with him in his childhood knew him not, he had grown so handsome. When the Sultan saw him he came down from his throne, embraced him, and led him into a hall where a feast was spread, intending to marry him to the Princess that very day. But Aladdin refused, saying, "I must build a palace fit for her," and took his leave. Once home, he said to the genie: "Build me a palace of the finest marble, set with jasper, agate, and other precious stones. In the middle you shall build me a large hall with a dome, its four walls of massy gold and silver, each having six windows, whose lattices, all except one which is to be left unfinished, must be set with diamonds and rubies. There must be stables and horses and grooms and slaves; go and see about it!"

The palace was finished by the next day, and the genie carried him there and showed him all his orders faithfully carried out, even to the laying of a velvet carpet from Aladdin's palace to the Sultan's. Aladdin's mother then dressed herself carefully, and walked to the palace with her slaves, while he followed her on horseback. The Sultan sent musicians with trumpets and cymbals to meet them, so that the air resounded with music and cheers. She was taken to the Princess, who saluted her and treated her with great honor. At night the Princess said good-by to her father and set out on the carpet for Aladdin's palace, with his mother at her side, and followed by the hundred slaves. She was charmed at the sight of Aladdin, who ran to recieve her. "Princess," he said, "blame your beauty for my boldness if I have displeased you." She told him that, having seen him, she willingly obeyed her father in this matter. After the wedding had taken place Aladdin led her into the hall, where a feast was spread, and she supped with him, after which they danced till midnight.

Next day Aladdin invited the Sultan to see the palace. On entering the hall with the four-and-twenty windows, with their rubies, diamonds, and emeralds, he cried: "It is a world's wonder! There is only one thing that surprises me. Was it by accident that one window was left unfinished?" "No, sir, by design," returned Aladdin. "I wished Your Majesty to have the glory of finishing this palace." The Sultan was pleased, and sent for the best jewelers in the city. He showed them the unfinished window, and bade them fit it up like the others. "Sir," replied their spokesman, "we cannot find jewels enough." The Sultan had his own fetched, which they soon used, but to no purpose, for in a month's time the work was not half done. Aladdin, knowing that their task was vain, bade them undo their work and carry the jewels back, and the genie finished the window at his command. The

Sultan was surprised to receive his jewels again, and visited Aladdin, who showed him the window finished. The Sultan embraced him, the envious Vizier meanwhile hinting that it was the work of enchantment.

Aladdin had won the hearts of the people by his gentle bearing. He was made captain of the Sultan's armies, and won several battles for him, but remained modest and courteous as before, and lived thus in peace and content for several years.

But far away in Africa the magician remembered Aladdin, and by his magic arts discovered that Aladdin, instead of perishing miserably in the cave, had escaped, and had married a princess, with whom he was living in great honor and wealth. He knew that the poor tailor's son could only have accomplished this by means of the lamp, and traveled night and day until he reached the capital of China, bent on Aladdin's ruin. As he passed through the town he heard people talking everywhere about a marvelous palace. "Forgive my ignorance," he said, "what is this palace you speak of?" "Have you not heard of Prince Aladdin's palace," was the reply, "the greatest wonder of the world? I will direct you if you have a mind to see it." The magician thanked him who spoke, and, having seen the palace, knew that it had been raised by the Genie of the Lamp, and became half mad with rage. He determined to get hold of the lamp, and again plunge Aladdin into the deepest poverty.

Unluckily, Aladdin had gone a-hunting for eight days, which gave the magician plenty of time. He bought a dozen copper lamps, put them into a basket, and went

143

to the palace, crying: "New lamps for old!" followed by a jeering crowd. The Princess, sitting in the hall of four-and-twenty windows, sent a slave to find out what the noise was about, who came back laughing, so that the Princess scolded her. "Madam," replied the slave, "who can help laughing to see an old fool offering to exchange fine new lamps for old ones?" Another slave, hearing this, said: "There is an old one on the cornice there which he can have." Now this was the magic lamp, which Aladdin had left there, as he could not take it out hunting with him. The Princess, not knowing its value, laughingly bade the slave take it and make the exchange. She went and said to the magician: "Give me a new lamp for this." He snatched it and bade the slave

take her choice, amid the jeers of the crowd. Little he cared, but left off crying his lamps, and went out of the city gates to a lonely place, where he remained till nightfall, when he pulled out the lamp and rubbed it. The genie appeared, and at the magician's command carried him, together with the palace and the Princess in it, to a lonely place in Africa.

Next morning the Sultan looked out of the window toward Aladdin's palace and rubbed his eyes, for it was gone. He sent for the Vizier and asked what had become of the palace. The Vizier looked out too, and was lost in astonishment. He again put it down to enchantment, and this time the Sultan believed him, and sent thirty men on horseback to fetch Aladdin in chains. They met him riding home,

144

bound him, and forced him to go with them on foot. The people, however, who loved him, followed, armed, to see that he came to no harm. He was carried before the Sultan, who ordered the executioner to cut off his head. The executioner made Aladdin kneel down, bandaged his eyes, and raised his scimitar to strike. At that instant the Vizier, who saw that the crowd had forced their way into the courtyard and were scaling the walls to rescue Aladdin, called to the executioner to stay his hand. The people, indeed, looked so threatening that the Sultan gave way and ordered Aladdin to be unbound, and pardoned him in the sight of the crowd. Aladdin now begged to know what he had done. "False wretch!" said the Sultan, "come hither," and showed him from the window the place where his palace had stood. Aladdin was so amazed that he could not say a word. "Where is my palace and my daughter?" demanded the Sultan. "For the first I am not so deeply concerned, but my daughter I must have, and you must find her or lose your head." Aladdin begged for forty days in which to find her, promising, if he failed, to return and suffer death at the Sultan's pleasure. His prayer was granted, and he went forth sadly from the Sultan's presence. For three days he wandered about like a madman, asking everyone what had become of his palace, but they only laughed and pitied him. He came to the banks of a river, and knelt down to say his prayers before throwing himself in. In so doing he rubbed the magic ring he still wore. The genie he had seen in the cave appeared, and asked his will. "Save my life, genie," said Aladdin, "bring my palace back." "That is not in my power," said

the genie; "I am only the Slave of the Ring; you must ask him of the lamp." "Even so," said Aladdin, "but thou canst take me to the palace, and set me down under my dear wife's window." He at once found himself in Africa, under the window of the Princess, and fell asleep out of sheer weariness.

He was awakened by the singing of the birds, and his heart was lighter. He saw plainly that all his misfortunes were owing to the loss of the lamp, and vainly wondered who had robbed him of it.

That morning the Princess rose earlier than she had done since she had been carried into Africa by the magician, whose company she was forced to endure once a day. She, however, treated him so harshly that he dared not live there altogether. As she was dressing, one of her women looked out and saw Aladdin. The Princess ran and opened the window, and at the noise she made Aladdin looked up. She called to him to come to her, and great was the joy of these lovers at seeing each other again. After he had kissed her Aladdin said: "I beg of you, Princess, in God's name, before we speak of anything else, for your own sake and mine, tell me what has become of an old lamp I left on the cornice in the hall of four-and-twenty windows, when I went a-hunting." "Alas!" she said. "I am the innocent cause of our sorrows," and told him of the exchange of the lamp. "Now I know," cried Aladdin, "that we have to thank the African magician for this! Where is the lamp?" "He carries it about with him," said the Princess. "I know, for he pulled it out of his breast to show me. He wishes me to break my faith with you and marry him, saying that you were beheaded by my

father's command. He is forever speaking ill of you, but I only reply by my tears. If I persist, I doubt not but he will use violence." Aladdin comforted her, and left her for a while. He changed clothes with the first person he met in the town, and having bought a certain powder, returned to the Princess, who let him in by a little side door. "Put on your most beautiful dress," he said to her, "and receive the magician with smiles, leading him to believe that you have forgotten me. Invite him to sup with you, and say you wish to taste the wine of his country. He will go for some and while he is gone I will tell you what to do." She listened carefully to Aladdin and when he left she arrayed herself gaily for the first time since she had left China. She put on a girdle and headdress of diamonds, and, seeing in a glass that she was more beautiful than ever, received the magician, saying, to his great amazement: "I have made up my mind that Aladdin is dead, and that all my tears will not bring him back to me, so I am resolved to mourn no more, and have therefore invited you to sup with me; but I am tired of the wines of China, and would fain taste those of Africa." The magician flew to his cellar, and the Princess put the powder Aladdin had given her in her cup. When he returned she asked him to drink her health in the wine of Africa, handing him her cup in exchange for his, as a sign she was reconciled to him. Before drinking, the magician made her a speech in praise of her beauty, but the Princess cut him short, saying: "Let us drink first, and you shall say what you will afterward." She set her cup to her lips and kept it there, while the magician drained his to the dregs and fell back lifeless. The Princess then opened the door to Aladdin, and flung her arms round his neck; but Aladdin put her away, bidding her leave him, as he had more to do. He then went to the dead magician, took the lamp out of his vest, and bade

the genie carry the palace and all in it back to China. This was done, and the Princess in her chamber only felt two little shocks, and little thought she was at home again.

The Sultan, who was sitting in his chamber, mourning for his lost daughter, happened to look up, and rubbed his eyes, for there stood the palace as before! He hastened thither, and Aladdin received him in the hall of the four-and-twenty windows, with the Princess at his side. Aladdin told him what had happened, and showed him the dead body of the magician, that he might believe. A ten-day feast was proclaimed, and it seemed

as if Aladdin might now live the rest of his life in peace; but it was not to be.

The African magician had a younger brother, who was, if possible, more wicked and more cunning than he. He traveled to China to avenge his brother's death, and went to visit a pious woman called Fatima, thinking she might be of use to him. He entered her cell and clapped a dagger to her breast, telling her to rise and do his bidding on pain of death. He changed clothes with her, colored his face like hers, put on her veil, and murdered her, that she might tell no tales. Then he went toward the palace of Aladdin, and all the people, thinking he was the holy woman, gathered round him, kissing his hands and begging his blessing. When he got to the palace there was such a noise going on round him that the Princess bade her slave look out of the window and ask what was the matter. The slave said it was the holy woman, curing people by her touch of their ailments, whereupon the Princess, who had long desired to see Fatima, sent for her. On coming to the Princess the magician offered up a prayer for her health and prosperity. When he had done, the Princess made him sit by her, and begged him to stay with her always. The false Fatima, who wished for nothing better, consented, but kept his veil down for fear of discovery. The Princess showed him the hall, and asked him what he thought of it. "It is truly beautiful," said the false Fatima. "It wants but one thing." "And what is that?" said the Princess. "If only a roc's egg," replied he, "were hung up from the middle of this dome, it would be the wonder of the world."

After this the Princess could think of nothing but the roc's egg, and when Aladdin returned from hunting he found her in a very ill humor. He begged to know what was amiss, and she told him that all her pleasure in the hall was spoiled for the want of a roc's egg hanging from the dome. "If that is all," replied Aladdin, "you shall soon be happy." He left her and rubbed the lamp, and when the genie appeared commanded him to bring a roc's egg. The genie gave such a loud and terrible shriek that the hall shook. "Wretch!" he cried, "is it not enough that I have done everything for you, but you must command me to bring my master and hang him up in the midst of this dome? You and your wife and your palace deserve to be burned to ashes, but that this request does not come from you, but from the brother of the African magician whom you destroyed. He is now in your palace disguised as the holy woman—whom he murdered. He it was who put that wish into your wife's head. Take care of yourself, for he means to kill you." So saying, the genie disappeared.

Aladdin went back to the Princess, saying his head ached, and requesting that the holy Fatima should be fetched to lay her hands on it. But when the Magician came near, Aladdin, seizing his dagger, pierced him to the heart. "What have you done?" cried the Princess. "You have killed the holy woman!" "Not so," replied Aladdin, "but a wicked magician," and told her of how she had been deceived.

After this Aladdin and his wife lived in peace. He succeeded the Sultan when he died, and reigned for many years, leaving behind him a long line of kings.

"The Real Princess," sometimes known as
"The Princess and the Pea,"
is little more than an anecdote.
However, it is so striking and at the same time so absurd,
that the Princess has become
a symbol for all delicate and extra-sensitive people.

The Real Princess

BY HANS CHRISTIAN ANDERSEN
Illustrated by LOWELL HESS

There was once a Prince who wished to marry a Princess; but then she must be a real Princess. He traveled all over the world in hopes of finding such a one; but there was always something wrong. Princesses he found in plenty; but he could not make up his mind that they were real Princesses, for now one thing, now another, seemed to him not quite right about them. At last he went back to his palace quite downcast, because he wished so much to have a real Princess for his wife, and he had not been able to find one.

One evening a fearful tempest arose. It thundered and lightninged, and the rain came down in torrents. Besides, it was as dark as pitch. All at once there was a violent knocking at the door, and the old King, the Prince's father, went out himself to open it.

It was a Princess who was standing outside. What with the rain and the wind, she was in a sad state; the water trickled from her hair, and her clothes clung to her body. She said she was a real Princess.

"Ah, we shall soon see about that!" thought the old Queen-mother. She gave no hint whatever of what she was going to do, but went quietly into the bedroom, took all the bed-clothes off the bed, and put three little peas on the bedstead. Then she laid twenty mattresses one upon another over the three peas, and put twenty feather-beds over the mattresses.

Upon this bed the Princess was to pass the night.

The next morning she was asked how she had slept. "Oh, very badly indeed!" she replied. "I have scarcely closed my eyes the whole night through. I do not know what was in my bed, but I had something hard under me, and am all over black and blue. It has hurt me so much!"

Now it was plain that this must be a real Princess, since she had been able to feel the three little peas through the twenty mattresses and twenty feather-beds. None but a real Princess could have had such a delicate sense of feeling.

So the Prince made her his wife, being now convinced that he had found a real Princess. The three peas were, however, put into the royal museum, where they are still to be seen, if they have not been stolen.

Notice that this is a true story.

152